DEEP
DEEP
DOWN

Also by Garrett Carr

The Badness of Ballydog
Lost Dogs

DEEP
DEEP
DOWN

GARRETT
CARR

SIMON AND SCHUSTER

First published in Great Britain in 2011 by Simon & Schuster UK Ltd
A CBS COMPANY

1 3 5 7 9 10 8 6 4 2

Simon & Schuster UK Ltd
1st Floor
222 Gray's Inn Road
London
WC1X 8HB

www.simonandschuster.co.uk

Simon & Schuster Australia, Sydney

Simon & Schuster India, New Delhi

A CIP catalogue copy for this book is available
from the British Library.

PB ISBN: 978-1-84738-600-7
E-BOOK ISBN: 978-1-84738-986-2

Printed and bound by CPI Group (UK) Ltd, Croydon CR0 4YY

1

The rain was loud but he still heard the *snap*. It sounded like part of the fence breaking. It was near midnight. Hard rain slammed down, each drop crashing against the roof and exploding. Through the window Ewan saw movement in the shrubbery at the back of the garden. A pale blur emerged, reflecting and shimmering in the drips running down the glass. The blur solidified into a person as it stepped closer. It was May.

Quietly, Ewan let her in and brought her to his room. This was his aunt's house and she did not approve of late callers. Or any callers, any time. But May came and went as she wished. She did not care about commonplace things, like the time. Now May was soaked and her dress was grass-stained. Only her wellington boots were sensible for the weather. She wrung out her hair and gazed around Ewan's room. They had not spoken since their last trip to see Andrew in hospital a month before.

'Give me some food, will ye,' said May.

'I've a dozen sandwiches packed in that bag,' said Ewan. 'Have them.'

'I'll need more than that,' said May, but she grabbed a sandwich out of the backpack lying on Ewan's bed. She peeked inside to make sure it was vegetarian then stuffed it in her mouth. They looked at one another as May chewed. They had both seen a lot of trouble recently. You could see it in Ewan's eyes. He had a lonely, orphaned look. You could detect it in May's arrogance. She held herself aloof from the ordinary.

'Planning on running away again?' she asked as she swallowed, pointing at the bag with her thumb.

'Yes,' said Ewan, 'if it ever stops raining.'

'Where will ye go?'

Ewan looked away. He had no plan. He had nothing but a desire to get away from here.

May started on a second sandwich. 'Didn't those Social Services people say that if ye went AWOL again they'd put ye in a *unit*?'

'Yes, a unit,' he said. 'Whatever that means.'

'I'll tell ye what it means,' said May. 'Nasty food and communal showers. Locked dorm rooms all filled with boys from broken homes.'

'I might fit in,' said Ewan.

May snorted. 'Ye would not,' she said. 'You're too soft. The other lads would have your guts out the

2

second ye said *please pass the butter* or some other bit of well-raised chat. So if you're goin' to run away ye better not get caught. Ye better come with us.'

'Not sure I can live with rabbits or foxes or whoever you run with these days,' said Ewan.

It was true that May wandered wild. She had been practising her talent with animals, spending days away from people, in forests or by remote coast. But May never went long without visiting Andrew, their wild friend. Going to visit him far more often than Ewan did. Andrew was being kept in a secure hospital. He was host to a ferocious infection that had reshaped him, made him half-monster.

'I'm here about Andrew,' said May. 'They want to operate. Rip those creatures out of him.'

'I heard,' said Ewan. 'They're going to do it this week. I guess it's the last chance he's got.'

'We can't let them cut him open,' said May. 'It'll kill him. Or leave him brain-damaged. Even the doctors say it's fierce dangerous.'

'Andrew will never be allowed home the way he is now,' said Ewan. 'And going home is the only thing he wants. I bet if he was able to understand, he'd choose to risk the operation. It's that or spend his life locked away. Andrew would rather take the gamble. Besides,' Ewan continued with a shrug, 'they're going to operate whatever we think. There's nothing we can do.'

3

Ewan considered himself a realist.

'Aye there is,' said May. She leaned forward, as if with a huge secret that others might overhear. 'We can get him out of hospital and take him to this lake I've heard about.'

'A lake?'

'It's somewhere in the mountains,' said May. 'Its water cures all ills.'

'Who told you about it?' asked Ewan.

'A wee bird,' laughed May.

Ewan waited.

'Actually, it was a bunch of swans I met by a river,' said May. She held her hands together as she remembered them. 'Ye should have seem them, Ewan. The most beautiful things ever. I'm sure I got good knowledge from them. They were hatched by the lake. Its water made them perfect. I reckon it could cure Andrew.'

May's ability to commune with animals was not always reliable. Ewan thought this lake sounded like a myth or exaggerated story. But May was so full of hope that he did not say so. Instead he gave a practical reason why the idea was a non-starter.

'The hospital will never let anyone take Andrew out,' said Ewan. 'Not even for an hour.'

'So break him out instead,' said May. 'Go visit and ask permission to bring Andrew for a walk around the grounds. You've seen the grounds, they're big.

Stroll a bit and get out of sight of the security cameras. Then, with some pointing and cajoling, get Andrew to rip open the boundary fence. Then make a run for it. Easy.'

'That fence is electrified,' said Ewan.

'IS IT?' exclaimed May. Her face snapped towards the window. Rain was hammering down outside, ricocheting off the windowsill. 'Andrew's so tough,' she said, dazed and impressed. 'He didn't complain. I don't think he even noticed.'

It took a moment to sink in.

Ewan leaped to the window. Even in the darkness he could see the garden had changed, taken on extra bulk. A sense of living presence out there made his heart thump. Something monstrous was in the night and the rain. The shape heaved in and out as it breathed. It was human-formed but bigger than a normal person, lumpy and crooked. Rain bounced off its wide shoulders. It was watching. It was waiting.

'I've already done it,' said May. 'I bust him out.'

'You're a kidnapper!' said Ewan.

She giggled, sounding both frightened and thrilled. 'I suppose I am,' she said. 'Do ye reckon they'll put *me* in a unit too?'

'This is serious.'

It was, and May knew it. 'He's our friend,' she said, 'and he's ill, *that's* serious. They want to rip out his infection and probably destroy him in the process,

5

that's serious. So, we have to do something. Like right now. These are serious times.'

Ewan looked out at Andrew and shook his head. 'Oh, May,' he said.

But ten minutes later they left. They had to make the most of the night. Andrew, the monster-boy, was impossible to hide. They walked through the suburbs and into the countryside.

Andrew loved the rain. *Rain = Good*. He loved it even as it drenched him. He had grown up by the sea but here was in an unfamiliar landscape of rolling hills and farmland. He had no idea where he was or where he was being taken. The rain was the single thing familiar to him. The single thing he had to remind him of home.

'Hooommee,' he murmured.

This was the only word Andrew still knew.

His big jaw worked from side to side. His skin was stretched tight over yawning ligaments. The rain drummed against it. His big arm swung. It ended at a slab of a hand and blunt fingers that almost touched the ground when uncurled. When he cracked his knuckles it sounded like gunfire. The other arm was not so big but was still packed with immense strength. He stopped and raised it now, pointing away westward.

When confused, Andrew could be dangerous. Andrew was often confused. He knew only two things. That he was a boy and not supposed to be this monster. And that he wanted to be at . . .

'HOOOMMEE,' he howled.

Ewan stopped and looked back. He did not bother going to Andrew but May was at his side in a flash. She reached up and put her hand on Andrew's out-stretched arm, still pointing to where he thought home might be. Andrew could not understand words but May spoke anyway.

'We're looking for a lake that'll cure ye,' she said. 'Then you'll be able to go home.'

To Andrew, voices were just noise but he had sharp instincts. He trusted May by her tone, her touch and the light of her eyes. *May = Good*. He followed her. He would follow her anywhere.

By morning they were in the foothills and there their problems really began. People did not react well to the monster-boy. Even from a distance, his tall crooked shape loping along a ridge caused loathing. Farmers stood in doorways with shotguns cradled in their arms and glared at them. They strayed too close to a village and a carload of men drove slowly behind them, herding the teenagers like beasts, until they were away. When such things happened, May became angry. So angry that all around badgers and hares snapped awake, gripped by her frustration. The animals kicked and scraped at their burrow's clay walls but there was nothing they could do.

7

May and Ewan led Andrew away from the roads, climbing among the hills. Not long after, they saw police cars going to and fro beneath them. From now on they would stick to high paths and empty bogland. There was nowhere to sleep so they would not sleep. May and Ewan walked ahead. Andrew lumbered behind.

Day one: hills and rain.

Day two: mountains and rain.

Ewan clambered up a slope, using the vantage point to see if they were being followed. No one. They were completely alone in this raw landscape. They were off the map.

'It's just us,' he called to May.

No human life. No wildlife, either.

May was looking skyward. She squinted against the rain and searched the sky for a swan or any other guide. Any animal that could lead them closer to the lake. But there was nothing in the air. The rain was too thick. Too relentless. The sun was reduced to a grey smudge in the sky. In the dark clefts of a cliff, May detected crows and a grumpy owl but none of them would help. Every creature was huddled against the malignant wet. Even their senses seemed waterlogged.

The trio kept walking. Ahead of them, looming forms emerged from the downpour. Their shapes hardened into a row of wind turbines. Each was seven storeys tall. Their blades were turning slowly. Andrew stopped and growled at them. Only six months before Andrew could have described the mechanism at work inside a wind turbine. He could have made a good guess at how much electricity they produced. But now these machines were just more of the strange and alarming things that populated the world. They were just another mystery that might turn out dangerous. They were just another fright.

May took Andrew by the arm and led him onwards.

'He probably thinks they're giants,' said Ewan.

'You're the one with monsters on the brain,' said May.

Andrew was really the one with monsters on the brain – Ewan had seen the X-rays – but he did not respond to May's remark. She sniped at him all the time now. He knew May was annoyed because everything was going wrong – they were soaked, had nowhere to shelter and had still not found the lake. None of these things troubled Ewan. They were searching a mountain range called Mourne in a county called Down for a lake that probably did not exist. *Go wrong* was what Ewan expected. *Go wrong* was what things usually did. He hunched against the rain and kept trudging. They were a couple of kidnappers, there was no turning around. They could only go on.

May felt a presence, watching. She stopped. Looking around, she could not see where it was coming from. She raised her arms in a ritualistic pose while Andrew and Ewan watched her. Ewan knew the pose was unnecessary, it was her mind that did the work. Recently May had taken to raising her arms like that because she thought it looked cool and mysterious. She was showing off. But it was hard to argue with May's high opinion of herself. Her ability was astounding.

Silently, May called the animal and it obeyed. Ewan gasped as it galloped out of the rain. Red deer were the biggest mammals in the country but he had only ever seen them on television. Until now. This one was a stag. High antlers and a thick coat made it look like a king. But many metres away it took fright, locked its knees and halted, going from full gallop to still as stone in two seconds. Stillness was the deer's camouflage. By staying motionless it faded into the muddy background. If he took his eyes off it, Ewan thought, he might never find it again. Nothing moved, nothing breathed. Then Andrew whined with sadness. He had just grasped why the deer had halted. It feared him.

'Never mind.' May spoke to Andrew in a gentle tone. 'It'll still lead us.'

They followed as the deer swift-footed it away. At intervals it would wait, grand as a monument, for the teenagers to catch up. Before they got too close it would spring on again. In this way they were led over wide bogland towards a range of hills shrouded in cloud. The deer bounded up a hillside. Its knees were well engineered, launching the deer on and on, never faltering. The humans clambered slowly behind, Andrew's shoulders dipping and rolling. It seemed Andrew might never get used to his big feet and awkward shape. The rain came on harder. Higher up the hill, the soil thinned and stone was exposed. The deer's hooves clopped against the granite. Buckets of rainwater washed down and rippled around Andrew, May and Ewan's ankles. The way got steep, steeper, then rounded off as they approached the top.

'We're close,' said May.

Job done, the deer galloped away. May watched it go with her arms raised in a pose of gratitude.

'Give your thanks,' she directed Ewan.

Ewan sighed. 'Thank you, deer,' he said.

The rain peeled back as the trio crossed the hilltop. Suddenly the ground was dry. Behind them the rain's end hung like a curtain, one side wet and one side not. Beneath them was a lake, a splendid blue disc held between granite hills. The hills looked like eggs, domes of grey rock all just like the one they were standing on. There were five hills in total. On the lower slopes, pine trees had been planted in neat rows. These plantations ran to the lakeshore apart from where fields and a village hugged it. The village was a friendly-looking collection of thatched cottages and small farms. Every garden overflowed with flowers, fruit and vegetables. From their high position Andrew, May and Ewan could see people's backs at work among the crops. Other villagers were leaning on gateposts or sitting on front doorsteps and having a chat. Their laughter carried up to where the teenagers stood. No rain was falling anywhere inside the valley. The cheerful scene was dappled in sunlight. Birds and bees flitted about. The pine plantations were overrun with squirrels. Swans were at rest in the middle of the lake.

'There are heaps of animals,' said May. She pressed her hands to her ears although that made no difference to the clamour in her head. The damp sniffles of the creatures outside the valley had been replaced with a joyous, although tuneless, blast of life. May had never experienced anything like this intensity before. It would accompany her as long as she remained in the valley.

Ewan stood entranced by the clear air and pretty village. He could see the square outlines of old cottage walls under the water. Over the years the lake had obviously expanded. It shimmered all around its perfect roundness. It was a dream lake. It was a dream valley. Yet it was real. Already the sun was drying Ewan's clothes.

'This place seems so . . . good,' he said.

'Bet it's not as nice as it seems,' said May.

Ewan did not reply. He was surprised to find himself

optimistic. Just a little, but definitely optimistic. They stood silent a while, gazing into the valley.

'Let's hope Andrew doesn't do anything violent,' said May. 'I wasn't expecting a village and people and all.'

'There's no going back now,' said Ewan.

That was how Andrew, May and Ewan came to find the lake and the people living on its shore. They would soon discover this valley was just as pleasant as it looked, every citizen thriving off the miraculous waters of the lake. This place was called Lough Linger. A valley where everyone had what they needed. Where front doors were always open and kettles always on. The people of Lough Linger were so kind and generous that even these three unusual visitors would be made welcome. Even the monster-boy.

But . . . there is a but.

These were the last days of Lough Linger. Soon those cottages would be crushed. This place would be littered with rubble and broken trees. It was the visitors who carried this terror with them. It was no coincidence that Andrew, May and Ewan were going to see the destruction of this valley.

They were going to cause it.

2

An old man was first to spot the visitors. He marched down his garden path and waved his cane at them.

May bristled and Andrew, feeling her tension, bared his teeth.

'See?' said May. 'It's just like everywhere else.'

'No, he's only greeting us,' said Ewan. Ewan was right.

'*Bonjour!*' the man called. 'Welcome to Lough Linger!' He swished his cane in a circle, emphasising his chirpiness. He did not flinch at the sight of Andrew, even though the boy's teeth were bared and gritted. The man took Andrew's clamped jaws as a friendly smile. 'We don't receive many day trippers,' the man said. 'Let me show you around.'

They strolled down to the shore. Or, rather, May, Ewan and the old man, Mr Swift, strolled. Andrew lumbered, big and thumping. When moving, Andrew always seemed to be accompanied by the clash of drums and heavy-metal guitars. He sucked in the smell of turf fires, baking bread and sawdust rising from a sawmill. He liked the smells. In the fields, workers straightened their backs and greeted the visitors with whatever happened to be in their hands, waving carrots and great rods of Brussels sprouts. Farmers smiled hello as they loaded a van to bring their produce to market. In the village, the gardens were in bloom. The visitors heard fiddle music coming through an open door. People stepped from their cottages, wiped their hands on their aprons and came forth to meet them.

'Will you have a wee cuppa?' enquired Mrs Hume. The thick lenses of her glasses made her eyes massive, the pupils seeming to float way out in front of her face. She grinned and blinked.

'Who have we here?' a lady enquired of Mr Swift. Her name was Miss Boswell. Her close-cropped hair made her look practical and efficient. The scent of almonds hung around her.

'Travellers from afar,' said Mr Swift. 'Maybe they've heard about your baking.'

Miss Boswell laughed, looking at him fondly.

Both women were as old as Mr Swift. It seemed everyone here was old. Not parent-old, but grandparent-old. They all wore slip-on shoes and woolly cardigans. Was this a retirement village?

'I've just made a batch of scones,' said Mrs Grace, her white hair gleaming.

15

'And I'll make us a big pot of tea,' said Mr Hopkins, his hairless head shining.

'Our friend has an infection and we'd like him to drink from your lake,' Ewan said to the dozen old folk now surrounding them. 'Would that be allowed?'

The villagers had been too polite to stare at the monstrous boy but now they felt it was permissible. They studied Andrew. May heard his muscles tighten. He did not like so many eyes on him. The last time he had been surrounded like this, it had been by a gang of hospital orderlies come to restrain him. That had ended in blood and tears, although none of it had been Andrew's.

'Drink from the lake?' said Betty Bird nervously. 'I'm not sure that's a good idea.'

'And why not?' asked Mr Swift.

Mrs Bird was embarrassed. 'They're outsiders,' she said.

'So what?' laughed Mr Swift. 'Our lake makes no distinctions. Visitors, lead the way!'

Other villagers were smiling encouragingly. They let the visitors through, then fell in behind. Mrs Bird gave in and scuttled after them. Despite their ages no one had difficulty keeping up, even the most wrinkly clipped along. More and more people came out of their homes and joined in. The visitors found themselves at the head of a procession walking towards the shore. May was relieved to see that not everyone was old after all. Adults of all ages were converging from the cottages, fields and workplaces. 'The big lad has an illness,' villagers explained over and over again as the procession swelled. 'Nothing better than to take our waters then so,' was agreed by all. Everyone was hopeful and happy to help. This was turning into a charming day out for everyone. Children skipped down lanes and joined the flow. Teenagers emerged and tagged along, whispering to each other and trying to get a look at the visitors.

Andrew pounded along between Ewan and May. He had cooled down now that everybody was out of his line-of-sight. It was May who had her shoulders hunched and wished everyone would go away. She did not want an audience present when Andrew was healed and became his old self again. He had become this monster-boy in order to save her life. It was fitting that May's ability had located the lake. It would also be fitting if they were alone together when he was cured.

As they passed the community centre, a young woman emerged. She had blonde curls and a sparkling smile. She stepped through the double doors like she was stepping out of a shampoo advert.

'Our Mayor,' announced Mr Swift, jabbing his cane in her direction.

'Welcome,' she said, twinkling. Her name was Amber Feather.

The lake was inviting but the village had only one

boat, a rowboat strung to the jetty. The jetty was as solid as the hills. It was built of granite blocks arranged with such care that not a single weed had found nook. The teenagers walked to the end of the jetty and climbed down the steps, Andrew having to shift sideways to get to the water's edge. The steps continued on down under the surface before fading into the deep. The lake smelled of crystal and light. Its surface was spread smooth and blue before them, the sky above was blue and even the hills across the lake shimmered in a blue haze. You might have called the view heavenly. Especially if you liked blue.

Ewan looked at Andrew meaningfully and pointed to the water. Andrew just whimpered and scraped his massive bare feet on the steps – no boot was big enough for Andrew. He seemed suddenly shy. You could lead a monster-boy to water but you could not make him drink.

'He doesn't like them ones watching,' said May, not caring if the villagers heard or not.

It was a short jetty but many had squeezed on it to watch. Ewan glanced up and caught the impression of friendly faces and curiosity. He saw Mrs Hume's big eyes blinking. A boy with red hair and a red face burrowed his way to the front and stared at the monster-boy, horrified and fascinated at the same time. Beside him, a man raised a camera to his eye and snapped a photo. 'For our local paper,' he explained.

Ewan forced a smile and turned back around. 'There's no danger of Andrew going on the rampage, is there?' he whispered to May.

'There's always danger of that,' she replied.

She went down to the next step, which was submerged. Standing on it, the water came almost to the tops of her wellingtons.

'Careful there,' Mr Hume advised from beside his wife. He stroked his white beard.

'Don't slip!' said Mrs Bird.

'They'll be fine,' said Amber Feather. She was watching with interest.

'Take a drink, Andrew,' said May, demonstrating by crouching down and scooping water up to her mouth. 'This could be your cure.'

Slowly Andrew got the message. *Drink Water = Good*. Without taking his eyes off May he got down on one knee. He did not scoop at the water, even though his bigger hand could have held a basin-load. He dropped his face straight into the lake and gulped.

Gulp, gulp. Glug.

Water coated his gums. It tasted like stone, mineral rich and heavy despite its clarity. It seemed to thicken in his throat and was difficult to get down.

Glug.

He swallowed harder.

Glug.

Andrew pulled his face out of the water and smacked

19

his lips. May smiled hopefully. He looked at her and felt a forgotten version of himself turn once inside his body, like a sleeper rolling over during a nightmare. For a moment he was human again, the details of his life and mind revealed to him. But an instant later his infection had dug back in. It was back to basics for Andrew, the monster-boy. *May = Good. Ewan = Good.* But he himself was not. He looked down at his own hands, they were still monstrous and misshapen. He prodded a thick vein in his forearm. It had not faded. Not even slightly. May's smile was still in place but its naturalness had fallen away from behind it. Now it was masking disappointment. Andrew looked at his reflection in the lake. He saw the same inarticulate face through the same yellow eyes. Shame burned his insides. He turned away from May.

'I knew it wouldn't work!' said the boy with the red hair and the red face.

'Tim, try to be nice,' said Miss Boswell.

Andrew saw everyone looking down at him, pitying him. He did not like that. It was better to be feared. But he did not like that, either. Ewan had to jump away as Andrew lifted his arms, closing his hands into two meaty lump hammers. His skin stretched taunt and each finger clamped into its hardest lock. Fists above his head, Andrew was like a loaded catapult. Loneliness filled his chest, was held for five seconds, then released in a roar.

HUOORRRRRRRR . . .

Villagers stepped back in unison, gripping each other for support. Betty Bird emitted a squeak of distress. The monster-boy's cry echoed around the valley and the swans took off in a loud bluster. He flung his fists down, slamming them into a stone step. It cracked open, releasing a hiss of ancient carbon. The shock rocked through the jetty. Stones hopped in a wave. Villagers were tossed sideways. The photographer dropped his camera and dented the lens. Two people fell into the water, yelling. The boy with the red hair and the red face toppled into the rowboat, bashed his head and lay there with his legs in the air.

The people of Lough Linger had never seen such chaos.

While May soothed the monster-boy, Ewan attempted a public relations rescue. 'We're sorry, we're sorry,' he said.

Villagers helped each other up. The boy in the rowboat was moaning and rubbing his head. The water was shallow around the jetty, people were wet but unhurt. The villagers were against these visitors now. The monster-boy had slumped on the lowest step, looking down between his feet. Having smashed a stone he was now subdued but he was obviously a rough sort, prone to acts of destruction. Vandalism; the people of Lough Linger did not approve of things like that.

Miss Boswell looked down the steps at the visitors. 'I think it's best if you all go home now,' she said.

Ewan was aware of one terrible fact. They had nowhere to go. But there was something else on Ewan's mind. Lush nature all around, the sunny atmosphere, the gentle people, Ewan liked it here. He wanted to stay longer. 'Don't be alarmed,' he said to the villagers, 'Andrew gets frustrated sometimes but he wouldn't hurt a fly.'

'A fly, no,' said Amber Feather, watching the misshapen boy with steady suspicion. 'Not a fly.'

The monster-boy might prefer bigger victims.

'Good may come of this yet,' Mr Swift suddenly announced. Everyone looked at him, wondering where his positive chime came from. Did he not see what had just happened?

'We were unreasonable to expect an instant cure,' Mr Swift went on. 'Maybe Andrew needs to take the waters over a number of days.'

'That could be it!' said Ewan.

There were grumbles from the crowd but Mr Swift tapped his cane, overruling them and then going further. 'Stay right here with us a while,' he said to Ewan. 'We even have a guest house, although it hasn't been used in years. Your friend can take the waters every day and we're sure to see an improvement.'

Mr Swift was known for his wild notions but this was the wildest yet. Many villagers were unhappy with the idea of a monster-boy among them. Andrew seemed temperamental and aggressive. He might break something. Someone's neck, for example.

'Now, now,' said Mr Swift, talking down the mutterings. 'We've been blessed by the lake, as were our parents, and their parents, and their parents before them. When we meet someone in need it's our duty to share. Don't tell me you disagree?'

Miss Boswell was looking at him, more sad than annoyed. 'Do you really think it's for the best?' she asked.

'Of course,' said Mr Swift. 'I'm certain the boy will behave himself from now on. Won't he?' He was looking at Ewan.

Ewan nodded eagerly.

The villagers shuffled on their feet. 'Aye, I suppose,' said Farmer Able eventually. He had a knobbly walking stick and wore a woolly hat that drooped to one side like a garden gnome's. 'Is only right to give the wains a go at the lake. Share and share alike!'

'You're right of course,' said Mr Hume, stroking his white beard.

'Yes, let them stay,' said Mrs Merriman, sorry that she had been against the idea, even for a minute.

The villagers had wavered but their decency won out in the end. The teenagers could stay. A little while anyway.

May stayed on the bottom step caring for Andrew but Ewan went up and joined the crowd.

'You did well to find us,' Carrick McCuddy said to Ewan. The old man's face was deeply lined. Anywhere else his eyes would be described as *kindly*, but here that was not unusual. Here it was the norm. Everyone's eyes were kindly. Not long ago Ewan might have found this odd, perhaps even suspicious. But today he was so refreshed by it that he ignored any doubts. Ewan now remembered his respectful, polite side. He used to be so polite that he was mocked for it. But it seemed no one mocked anyone in Lough Linger.

'Will you have that cuppa?' asked Mrs Hume.

'Oh, yes please,' said Ewan.

'What will the visitors do all day?' asked Betty Bird. 'We're not used to guests around the place.'

May looked up from the bottom step. An alarm bell was going off in her mind, or rather a school bell. She had already seen the schoolhouse on the far side of the village. She did not need to get any closer. 'Don't worry, we'll stay out of your way,' she offered quickly. But that went down heavily among the villagers. It sounded so unfriendly.

'What ages are you?' asked Mr Swift.

'We're all fifteen,' said Ewan and he saw May flash him a look. This look consisted of a flare to her brow, a disappointed deflation in her shoulders and, with her mouth, the sort of shape you might make when presented with something truly stupid. The look lasted only a split second but managed to say, *Ye've gone and told them our ages. Now they'll make us go to school. Eejit.*

Sure enough, Mr Swift said, 'We'll be glad to school you while you're with us. We can't have you telling the outside world that the citizens of Lough Linger failed in their moral and legal duty to educate you.'

'Great,' said May.

She looked out over the lake. The lake that had failed to heal Andrew. The view was tranquil but inside she raged. It had taken all her skill to bring them here. Was this her reward? A pat on the head and to be told to keep trying? They had walked many miles through tough country and what had it brought them? A bunch of wrinklies with a tea addiction and, worst of all, a school.

3

The schoolhouse was a whitewashed building with a yellow thatch. Fruit trees grew all around it, everyone ate from them at break times. There were plenty of break times. The halls were wallpapered in paintings of lake views and sunny scenes. The staff were supportive and patient. May did not like it one bit.

She kept her back to the classroom wall and scanned the place. It was completely unlike anywhere May had ever been. No animal on earth was stranger to her than these teenagers. She knew about nastiness, not niceness. Her mam had left her. Her dad had neglected her. Her school had treated her roughly. But instead of loving the fresh, friendly atmosphere of this school, it actually upset her. She felt excluded by it. Such a place could not be for her. May had been beamed up to an advanced civilisation. She did not like it here. She could not speak their language.

Keeping as far as possible from the blackboard, May sat on the last bench. It creaked as it took

Andrew's weight beside her. Ewan slid in next to them and looked around. There was woodwork equipment and a stack of rough logs for sculpting. There were microscopes, computers, cases of fossils. The blackboard carried traces of lessons gone by: algebra, French verbs and the names of Jupiter's moons. Ewan liked it. It seemed like a room where anything and everything could be learned.

The other students were fascinated by the new-comers. They gathered around them. There was no uniform but they all wore the same bleached cuffs and pastel-hued pullovers. They all had perfect skin, well-defined cheekbones and twenty-twenty vision. They were the result of generations of enough exercise, enough sleep, enough milk and enough honey. The boys looked like girls. The girls looked like angels.

A girl was gazing at Ewan wide-eyed. 'Are you in one of those boy-bands from the radio?' she asked.

May scoffed at her. 'Aye he is,' she said, 'and I'm the president.'

The girl backed off.

'May!' said Ewan. 'She was only curious.'

Ewan was taken by the class's grace and openness. There was no bullying, everyone was entitled to speak and everyone knew how to listen. Ewan did not care what May thought, he was glad they were going to this school. He would try to fit in. He looked at the unblemished students, wanting to speak but not knowing what to say.

No one noticed because everyone's attention was on Andrew. They examined his fleshy ears and bulging arms. Andrew hunched down, his chin almost on the desk. He was embarrassed that he might smell bad. It had never bothered him before but he suddenly hated the hairs sticking out of his hands. He put them under the desk and made two fists.

Tim, the boy with the red hair and the red face, was outside showing off the bruise on his forehead, gotten when Andrew's outburst knocked him from the jetty. Many of the students had witnessed this outburst. But they were unafraid. They were too innocent to realise that Andrew might still be dangerous. They gathered around him.

'Look!' one exclaimed. 'See the black veins in his arms!'

'One arm is bigger than the other!'

'Those teeth! I'd say he'd bite through anything.'

Their faces pressed closer. Andrew clenched his fists harder. The students were like lambs frolicking around a minefield.

'He's brilliant,' they all agreed.

'Don't mind Tim,' one boy said to Ewan and May. 'He's delighted with his injury. It gives him a chance to be centre of attention. He loves that. I'm surprised he's been made a Bride.'

'A Bride?' said Ewan. Then he got a sinking feeling. *CRACK*.

Bent to its limit, the bench snapped under Andrew's weight. The three of them hit the floor. Andrew whined, he had made a fool of himself again. He sat up and shook his shoulders. But before Andrew's humiliation sank in, something happened to distract him. Their teacher entered, tapping his cane against his polished shoe with the beat of his step. They should have guessed, the teacher was Mr Swift.

'My, my,' he said, 'you're built like a tank.' He looked at the bench, then at Andrew again. 'No matter, you've given us a fine project on which to base a woodwork lesson. In fact, I'm grateful to you. Thank you, Andrew, thank you. We shall repair this seat of learning, practising the art of the dovetail and studying the principles of tensile strength.'

Endearingly, Mr Swift spoke directly to Andrew, although it was obvious Andrew could not understand him. He made a guttural noise, wanting to please the teacher. The monster-boy's instincts were warm to Mr Swift. He smelled nice and the noises that came out of his mouth were melodious. *Old Man With Stick = Good*.

'What are your impressions of Lough Linger?' Mr Swift asked Andrew. Andrew just grunted but the teacher detected some positivity in it. 'Good, good,' he said.

'It seems very homely,' offered Ewan.

'Too sheltered and safe,' said May. 'I prefer the real world.'

'Lough Linger is safer than most places,' Mr Swift agreed, 'but one is always wise to take care. Andrew for example.' He turned his attention to the monster-boy again. 'Might your temper be dangerous?'

Andrew just blinked.

'Aye it might,' said May with relish, 'Andrew can go demented.'

But, in contradiction of May's words, Mr Swift had stepped up to the monster-boy and was examining him closely. He studied his shoulders and looked up his dilated nostrils. Andrew leaned away from him, gritting his teeth. Andrew liked this brisk old man but he did not like being touched by anyone, except maybe May.

'Have you . . .' Mr Swift said to him, trying to be delicate, 'ever seriously hurt anyone?'

'How dare ye!' spluttered May. 'What do ye know, stuck away in this place? Ye don't know what life's been like for us. Andrew never bashed anyone that didn't deserve it.'

Just then the scent of vanilla entered. A girl stepped into the classroom, so lightly she seemed afloat. All the students rose from their benches. The newcomers were already standing as their bench was in two pieces on the floor. Mr Swift held his hands behind his back and straightened up. Why? These marks of respect confused May and Ewan. This girl was just another student and, besides, she was late. The girl did have a certain air about her. She was dressed in flowing white linen and had flowers in her hair. 'I am sorry I am late, Mr Swift,' she said. 'I had duties with the Founder.' Her voice was a whisper, it would have been inaudible in a normal classroom.

'Of course,' said Mr Swift.

She gazed upon the visitors, her face as neutral as the calm lake waters. May folded her arms and resisted but Ewan felt himself giving way under her eyes. The girl was so delicate, she might have been made of powder. Yet there was strength in her self-possession. She was used to being important. Doors opened before her, she had only to give them a glance.

The girl's eyes stopped on Andrew. She looked him up and down, taking in his warped but impressive frame. She inhaled softly. 'Welcome to Lough Linger,' she said.

'He doesn't understand ye,' May told her.

The girl placed a hand over her heart and inclined her head. There was a long moment of stillness. She had all the composure of a holy icon, a saint painted in zinc and gold leaf. Her lips hardly moved as she said, 'How sad.'

'Don't worry about it,' said May, 'I don't understand any of ye and I couldn't give a ****.'

A landmine had gone off. Bits of lambs were blasted to the ceiling, metaphorically speaking. These students were never exposed to such crude talk. They swooned into each other's arms. One boy began to cry.

Bad language; the people of Lough Linger did not approve of things like that.

4

Mr Swift did his duty at the time of May's explosive remark. He did not punish her, there was no punishment in Lough Linger, but he advised her that speaking correctly would gain her respect. It was later at home that he allowed himself to smile about the girl's coarse ways. Privately, Mr Swift thought it no harm to shake up the young minds of Lough Linger. No harm to rattle their cages. Mr Swift had enjoyed May's rage. She was rough but sincere.

He hung his cane on its hook inside his front door. Selecting some vegetables for his dinner, Mr Swift thought of Andrew. The boy was a marvel. He could break stones and roar like thunder. But could he be truly dangerous? May had reacted angrily to Mr Swift's enquiry. That made him think he was probably right. Andrew was dangerous. Maybe even a killer.

While the soup simmered, Mr Swift went to his armchair. He lifted the heaviest book off the shelf next to him. This English dictionary was probably the biggest in the valley. Chatting amongst themselves of agreeable things, as they did day and night, the citizens of Lough Linger used a narrower vocabulary than the rest of the world. They never needed the word 'desperation'. They never felt the urge for 'revenge'. They never tasted 'bitterness'.

But Mr Swift knew those words. He knew those words and many like them.

The dictionary opened where it always did, the page where a flower was pressed. A flower so dry and old it was almost transparent. Mr Swift gazed at it. He longed to lift it in his hand, just like he used to. But some time ago Mr Swift decided the flower was too delicate. Touch it and it might fall to pieces. He had not dared lift it in years.

It was given to him by a girl named Molly. He kept it in the dictionary by the word 'Love'.

Time had worn down Mr Swift's grieving, made its edges less sharp, like a river washing over a rough stone and making it smooth. But it was still a heavy grey presence that underlay his whole personality. Making him different from the other citizens of Lough Linger.

There was a tap on his door and a cheery, 'Good afternoon.' Miss Boswell let herself in. The people of Lough Linger rarely stood on doorsteps, at least during the day. They merrily walked in and out of each other's houses.

'That smells delicious and nutritious,' said Miss Boswell, referring to the soup bubbling on the stove. 'Look, I've bought some almond fingers for your afters.' They were stacked on a plate in her hands.

'How kind,' said Mr Swift. He knew Miss Boswell wanted an invite to stay for dinner. She often showed up like this. But Mr Swift preferred to eat alone, reading.

Miss Boswell saw the pressed flower in the dictionary. 'Oooh!' she said, a sad little exclamation.

Mr Swift closed the book. 'You don't approve of me inviting the outsiders to stay a while, do you?' he asked.

Miss Boswell looked down at the almond fingers. 'The ill boy needs help, anyone can see that,' she said, 'but we aren't good at keeping secrets here. We've had no practice. The longer the visitors stay, the more chance they'll discover our tradition. They wouldn't understand it. It might upset them.'

'*Upset* could be a reasonable reaction,' suggested Mr Swift.

'Don't say that,' said Miss Boswell. She put the almond fingers down and made rapidly for the door. She did not want to hear such disloyal talk. The more she heard, the more she would feel compelled to tell someone. The Mayor would be sure to find out in the end. Miss Boswell was too fond of Mr Swift to want that. At the door she stopped and said, 'We all loved Molly, you know. She was my classmate. But it was so many years ago. Will you ever move on? You're surrounded by people who care about you. Can't you let us in? Even just one of us?'

Miss Boswell hurried away. Mr Swift opened the dictionary and looked at the flower again. He looked at it a long time, forgetting about his soup until it boiled over and burned on the stove.

. . . grass . . . babies . . . lap . . . we . . . chew . . . grass . . . swoop . . . call . . . be . . . soar . . . dig . . . dig . . . care . . . dare . . . reach . . . chase . . . swim . . . chew . . . swim . . . stop . . . call . . . sing . . . bark . . . chase . . . care . . . reach . . . build . . . allow . . . dance . . . chew . . . mmmm . . . seek . . . dig . . . hold . . . nip . . . dance . . . feed . . . dark . . . sniff . . . nose . . . lick . . . clean . . . lay . . . attend . . . sing . . . birth . . . feed . . . still . . . move . . . nibble . . . mmmm . . .

Most visitors would be struck by Lough Linger's peace. But it was the noisiest place May had ever been. Animal life, both wild and farmed, was abundant and each creature was full of shrill vitality. After a couple of days in the valley May was becoming acclimatised. But there was no getting away from it, indoors and out, Lough Linger was loud.

Andrew, May and Ewan were in the guest house. Everything about the house was warm, old and somehow affectionate. The television was black and white and had a thick curved screen. Enamel utensils hung from bars above the table. The beds had tall wooden headboards. The guest house overlooked thatched roofs and beyond out to the lake. Of all the houses in the village it was furthest from the shore and highest up the valley's side. Directly behind it a pine plantation began. The creak of trees could be heard from the bedrooms.

Ewan gazed at the heavy roof beams and the thick walls. 'Homely,' he said every ten minutes.

Andrew was sitting on the floor nearby. May was standing behind him and combing his hair with her fingers. He liked that.

They were startled by a face at the window. A red face with red hair – it belonged to that boy Tim. He was only a couple of years younger than they were but he hopped around like an imp. Andrew growled at him, perhaps alarmed by his redness.

'I'm all fixed up,' he called through the glass. He lifted his hair to reveal a blemish-free forehead. It was incredible. That black bruise and bump should not have melted away so soon.

Ewan approached the window. 'How?' he asked.

'Drinking from the lake, how else?' said Tim. 'No one is ever sick or hurt here. Unless you're beyond help of course.'

Ewan knew why Tim had come here. To taunt

them. Drinking from the lake was not helping Andrew at all.

'It's got to do with your *soul*,' Tim went on. 'Some people's just aren't good enough. Hey—'

Crash.

Clatter.

May had thrown a saucer at the window. It cracked the windowpane and fell in five pieces. Tim hopped away, shouting, 'I'm only telling the truth!'

Andrew was up, agitated by the aggression in the air. May took him by the arm. 'We'll show him,' she said to Andrew. 'Let's go get ye another drink.'

The three visitors walked through the village. Workers were busy in the fields. Betty Bird's hair salon was open for trims, perms and purple rinses. There was an ante-natal class going on in the community centre – Lough Linger did not have a doctor or a nurse but it did have a midwife.

In the village shop Ewan picked up a copy of the *Bugle*, Lough Linger's newspaper. It only had half a dozen pages. The printer, journalist and photographer were all the same person. One word made up this week's headline: 'Visitors.' In the black-and-white picture May and Ewan were standing either side of Andrew. But the journalist had failed to get all of Andrew in. The top of his head was cut off. You could only see his big chin and gritted teeth trying to make a smile. Ewan looked through the rest of the paper. It was all good news.

The villagers they met were as generous as ever. On the way to the shore they were invited into people's homes for tea and biscuits about seventeen times.

'No ta,' said May to each invitation. 'We're taking Andrew for a drink.'

'Do we have to be in such a hurry?' Ewan asked her.

'Is there nothing ye like better than nattering to grannies?' said May.

On the jetty two old men were hoisting the village's rowboat up out of the water. They were two brothers and they were mighty friendly, chatting to the visitors while they flipped the rowboat upside down on the jetty stones. Hand-painted lettering on the bow said the boat was the *Bridal Sweet*.

The brothers Earlly were tough to tell apart, they had the same sharp noses and watery eyes. Ewan could see no obvious way to distinguish them. Some villagers claimed the best way was to check the position of their feet. The first brother was more forward while the second tended to hold back. Having lived long lives together, the brothers Earlly hardly needed to speak to one another anymore. When something occurred to one he would keep it to himself, thinking it out from both their perspectives. When he was done he would simply inform the other of the conclusion they had both arrived at. The brothers Earlly were actually born triplets but only two remained. Could they now be called twins? Nobody was sure.

'We're going to repaint the boat,' the first brother said to Ewan, although it was gleaming already. The hull had not picked up any stains or algae, such was the purity of Lough Linger. 'But first we'll do some fishing,' said the second brother.

May and Ewan led Andrew down the jetty steps. Andrew looked discomfited at the smashed step, remembering it was his handiwork. At the bottom he looked to his friends, down at the water, then back at his friends. His mind made another chunky recollection. *Drink Water = Good*. Andrew knelt down to the lake. He found the water difficult to swallow. It fizzed on his tongue.

May stood next to him and looked out over the water. She felt fish patrolling the lake floor beneath, rubbing against each other in the dark.

. . . nibble . . . mmmm . . . nibble . . . mmmm . . . nibble . . . mmmm . . . nibble . . . mmmm . . . nibble . . . mmmm . . .

The fish of Lough Linger were as content as its people.

'What are ye doing!'

Surprised, Ewan looked up from his cupped hands. May was glaring at him. He was kneeling down, drinking from the lake. 'What does it look like?' he said.

'Ye aren't sick,' said May.

Ewan sat up, bemused that his drinking from Lough Linger was so troubling to May.

'You don't have to be sick,' he said. 'Everyone here drinks it every day.'

'Aye and everyone here is weird,' said May. 'Shiny and jolly all the time. It's not natural. And this lake is the root of it. Andrew needs help but we're fine and shouldn't be drinking that stuff. Ye don't know what's in it.'

'If it's as powerful as they say then I want to experience it,' said Ewan. 'Besides, you have to drink water to stay alive and the taps in all the cottages are piped up from this lake. So you're drinking it whether you like it or not. But try the water here, it tastes best direct from the source.'

It had not occurred to May that the tap water came from the lake. She grumbled and folded her arms. The water in the guest house tasted good. In fact, it tasted wonderful.

'I'll not drink it straight anymore,' said May. 'I'll boil it and take it in me coffee.'

The fizzing in Andrew's throat made him splutter. He knelt back and growled at the water. He saw that Ewan had no difficulty drinking, that he was lapping happily from his cupped hands. An instinct reverberated through Andrew – this lake did not like him. But Andrew was used to things not liking him. Very little did these days.

41

5

May marched. She went into a pine plantation. The trees were planted in neat rows and close together. Place a hand against one trunk and, with your other hand, you could reach out and touch another. Walk around in a circle and you could touch four. There was no undergrowth, years of falling pine needles had layered up into a thick blanket that allowed nothing else to grow. It even kept sound down, muffling May's footsteps. The only noise was creaking from above. The pines were slender and exceedingly tall. A breeze made their tops sway back and forth, all of them always in parallel and creaking the whole time. They were like the masts of boats, swaying to the same tide.

May had a flashback – it was a memory she had never remembered before. She had been raised on a boat and sometimes, as a child, she'd stood with her chin against the mast and looked straight up. The mast seemed steady, although in reality it was slowly rocking with the rest of the boat. This made the clouds beyond the mast's tip seem to rove back and forth, like magic. She had always liked that. It was, May now supposed, a happy memory. Then her dad interrupted, just like he might have done in real life, by strolling onto deck. He would be saying something like, 'We're a good team, aren't we?' as he patted her, too hard, on the back. Then he would leave for town. Even as a small child May knew he was covering something up. Even as a child she knew he would come back drunk. Or not come back at all.

May focused on the present.

The way became higher and steeper, May was leaning into each step and ascending. High above the lake she emerged from the plantation, the soil thinned until there was none at all. She walked over the dome of the raw granite hilltop. This hilltop, like the other four around Lough Linger, was smooth and almost perfectly round. It was like walking on a small moon. Below, May could see the village. It looked like a toy town from up there. All around, she could see the Mountains of Mourne and the rain falling on them. This community was certainly hidden away. There had been no other visitors since they arrived. Work or business sometimes sent villagers out of the valley but they were never gone for long. People read papers or watched television news, but only so they could agree with each other about how terrible the outside world was and how lucky they were to have this marvellous valley.

May shuddered. A stiff cold breeze was blowing in from the mountains. Sometimes gusts whipped in rain but it mainly did not fall beyond an unnaturally sharp line around the valley edge. May stood in the dry and reached one hand into the normal world. Big cold droplets plopped into her palm.

May dropped her hand, startled. A girl had appeared and was standing just within the border between wet and dry. May did not recognise her from the school. She had silvery hair. She was wearing a cream-coloured mackintosh coat that flapped in the breeze. Around her neck she wore a pair of goggles, like an old-fashioned aviator. Strangest of all, she had a cricket bat. She was leaning on the bat and looking down on Lough Linger as if planning to invade it. Suddenly shy, May did not say anything but stood there, waiting for something to happen. The girl ignored her. On this barren dome there was no way she had not seen May. She was just too cool to be the first to speak.

'Hi,' said May at last. 'I'm May.'

The girl cast her eyes over May then resumed her study of Lough Linger. May waited, glancing at the girl in the mackintosh now and then. She had the posture and fine features of a Lough Linger teenager but was scruffy, like she might be sleeping rough. The boots she wore were dirty.

'Do ye live in the village?' May asked.

'I don't live with *those* people,' she said, 'not anymore.'

'Oh.'

'Look at them,' the girl went on, 'I can't tell the difference between the people and the sheep.'

Below, May could see villagers working in their fields and gardens. The two old brothers were fishing off the jetty. She could see flocks of sheep too, munching grass.

'Have ye come back for a visit?'

'You could say that,' the girl said, with a look so dark it made May avert her eyes. May looked instead towards the outside world, its rain and cold mountains. While walking to Lough Linger that landscape had seemed normal but now, compared to the sun-kissed valley they had discovered, it was miserable and grey.

'Did ye walk here too?' May asked.

'I never walk,' said the girl. She did not elaborate, trying to be mysterious probably. Instead she said, 'I was watching from up here when you first arrived. Your big retarded friend sure caused a fuss.'

'Andrew's not retarded!' said May. 'He's got an infection, that's all!'

'*Sorrieeee*,' said the girl, obviously not sorry.

But even though the girl irritated her, May did not want to leave her. They looked down into the valley again. The air was clear. The lake reflected the sky so impeccably that it actually looked like sky itself. It was as if the earth was flat, as people once believed, and someone had cut a circular hole in it.

'How did you find this place?' the girl asked.

'A wee bird told me,' said May and she said no more. Two could play at being mysterious.

'That's nice,' the girl said, but she was looking at May with interest now. 'My name is Theodora.'

'Nice name.'

'Do birds often tell you things?'

'Aye,' said May, 'but they're not so chatty as dogs.'

'As soon as I saw you I thought you'd something supernatural about you,' said Theodora. 'I knew because of your spaced-out look, your aloneness and . . . your wellingtons.'

'Don't care what ye think of me wellies,' said May. 'I like them, they're me *thing*.'

'Every girl needs a *thing*,' said Theodora, watching May closely. 'I suppose these goggles are mine.'

'I thought it was goin' to be the cricket bat,' said May.

'No,' said Theodora. 'The bat's temporary. I've nearly worn it out already.'

A gust hit them from across the mountains and Theodora's mackintosh was blown horizontal. The cutting air brought a gleam to her eye. Her silvery hair whipped and waved. They looked at each other for a few seconds, each pretending they were not freezing cold and did not need to seek shelter.

'Ye have something supernatural about ye, too,' said May.

'Are you saying I look weird?' Theodora said sharply.

'NO . . . sorry,' stammered May, 'just, ye look . . . magical.'

Theodora laughed. She had only been messing. May was relieved.

'Tell me yours and I'll tell you mine,' said Theodora.

May stepped closer. 'I commune with animals,' she said. 'We experience and learn things through each other. Right now I can feel every animal within two hundred metres. We're like, bonded.'

Theodora regarded her. She was not as impressed as May would have liked.

'Anything else?' Theodora asked.

'Of course not,' said May, stepping back. 'That's plenty, isn't it? Nobody ever has more than the one ability.'

'I have several,' said Theodora. She said it mildly but knew well that the idea was shocking.

May's amazement quickly gave way to disbelief. She raised a suspicious eyebrow.

'Most of them are useless,' Theodora explained. 'I can glow in the dark but what would be the point? My eyes have an extra-wide colour spectrum, so I can see colours ordinary people can't. But that's just a head-ache, mainly. I have one ability though that's better than all the rest put together.' She looked at May smugly. 'You're going to be jealous.'

May found herself leaning in. 'What is it?'

'I can fly.'

'Ye cannot!'

'Can.'

'I don't believe ye.'

'Don't believe me then.'

Theodora turned away and resumed her observation of Lough Linger, suddenly as remote as when May had first seen her. It was obvious Theodora would not fly just to impress someone. May had pushed it too far and now she regretted it. A flying girl would have been something to see, assuming Theodora was telling the truth. She might not be. People lied.

'I never met anyone with more than one ability,' said May. 'You're lucky.'

'It's nothing to do with luck,' Theodora said eventu-ally. 'I was born with only one ability, like you. But that first ability was about *taking things*. I'm able to capture other girls' powers. That's how I've collected so many.' Theodora turned on May, flexing her fingers and snatching into the wind with them. 'I take them and use them for myself.'

It took May a second to realise the implication of

this. Then fear hit her like a lightning bolt. She jumped away. Theodora smirked at her and made another pantomime grab at the air. May quick-stepped back, tripped over her wellingtons and bumped to the ground.

Theodora laughed and lowered her hands. 'Don't worry,' she said. 'It doesn't work like that. The girl has to *want* me to extract her power. I can't just steal it. It has to be given. She has to open herself up to the process.'

She offered her hand to help May up. May did not take it. She stayed on the ground. 'But who'd want to give away an amazing power?' she demanded.

'You'd be surprised,' said Theodora. 'Plenty of them do. Even the woman who could fly was glad to meet someone who could remove the ability. She'd been married to some bloke twenty years and never told him what she could do. She was ashamed of it.'

'That's crazy,' said May, although she knew that if she had not gotten free of her dad she would have grown up to be like that too. She would still be in her hometown, frightened of the voices in her head.

May accepted Theodora's hand and was pulled to her feet.

'Shame is often what helps me spot a girl with an ability,' explained Theodora. 'Look for the solitary old woman with a dozen cats. Or the strange girl in the pub that nobody speaks to. Or the timid girl walking home alone. Speak to them and sometimes, rarely of course, but sometimes, she'll be one of us.'

May found her heart thrilling to be in an 'us' with this girl. It must have shown because Theodora smiled back at her. With a flick of her wrist Theodora tossed the cricket bat into the air and caught it with both hands. She held it flat, like a tray.

'This bat is made from wood,' said Theodora, 'wood from a tree that spent forty years growing. Imagine, all those years of energy pushing through these fibres as the tree reached up and up. Energy that was constant although creeping and slow. But when I'm in contact with wood I can focus that energy and bring it out in a rush. It's not really me that flies, it's the timber. I just make it fly. And then I hang on.'

In one motion Theodora jumped, raised her knees, and threw the cricket bat under her feet. There was no return-to-ground slam. The bat stayed up. Theodora, standing on it like it was a skateboard, stayed up too. She extended her arms until balance was achieved then put her hands on her hips. Beneath the bat was a metre of empty air. By working her hips Theodora made herself rock back and forth, showing off. She grinned, mistress of the air.

'See you around,' Theodora called as she rocketed away, her mackintosh and silvery hair streaming out behind her. She was soon a grey shape in the rain.

May stared until Theodora had disappeared completely. Amazing.

May sat. She rested her chin in her hands and looked down into the valley. Theodora was right. It was hard to tell the difference between the people and the sheep.

6

Everywhere Ewan walked, villagers invited him into their homes. He had, in total, nine cups of tea, fifteen biscuits, six slices of toast and two of Mrs Grace's scones. Ewan worked out why he liked the company of the elderly, apart from the fact they fed him. It was because they saw him as adult. They were not just treating him as an adult, they genuinely saw an adult when they looked at him. From their aged point of view Ewan belonged in the same wide category as many older people. They did not distinguish between a fifteen-year-old and a twenty-five-year-old, just like he did not distinguish between people who were seventy and eighty. So they spoke to him as an equal, some perhaps even more so. The oldest folk hardy ever ventured to the outside world. Some had not left the valley in decades. They felt that Ewan, because he was from there, had qualifications they did not. They asked his opinion on the big news stories of the day and seemed to learn from his answers.

'All that trouble and turmoil,' they said, shaking their heads.

Sometimes Ewan found himself exaggerating the badness out there. He did not like to be dishonest and would stop himself with a mouthful of toast. But there was something comforting about these people. He liked their crinkly eyes and thoughtfulness. They made him want to pour his heart out. Ewan knew there was another reason an occasional exaggeration slipped out. He did not want to be sent away too soon.

'I think your valley is wonderful,' said Ewan. He meant it.

Villagers were pleased at that. They would brush the crumbs off their aprons and try not to look too proud. Ewan asked them about the community's remoteness. 'We keep ourselves to ourselves,' every-one told him. When he asked about the lake, villagers said that it was a blessing and they hoped that in the future more and more people would get to drink from it.

'From what you're saying, people might need it,' said Miss Boswell, 'but I suppose you're used to the outside world. It's where you belong. Don't you think you'd be happier out there?'

'Ah . . . I am not sure,' said Ewan.

Miss Boswell offered him another almond finger. Ewan declined. He knew she wanted them gone and the sooner the better.

Ewan decided that was enough tea for one afternoon.

He went through the village and slipped into the empty community centre. It had a church atmosphere, but not from any religion that Ewan recognised. Daubed across the floor and over the chairs were patches of pretty blue light. The light was projected from the stained glass window in the back wall above the podium. The window's picture was of a round lake among hills, Lough Linger most likely. Emerging from the water was a massive hand. It was a human hand, four fingers and a thumb, and with an open palm. Glass waterfalls were falling from it. Ewan imagined the giant person who would have to own such a hand, standing on the bottom of the lake and reaching up. Concentric ovals of glass radiated from the wrist, representing ripples on the lake surface. Standing on the palm was a boy in white robes. He looked down on Ewan with painted eyes. Eyes that were forever open – steady, forgiving and placid. This perfect boy was the community's centrepiece and he accepted his role with serenity. Ewan looked at him a long time. He was drawn to the image, drawn into it. He almost swam in it.

'That window's over a hundred years old,' said a voice.

Ewan turned. Amber Feather, Mayor of Lough Linger, was leaning against the door jamb. She might have been there for ages. She had a mischievous sparkle about her.

'It's . . . beautiful,' said Ewan.

'Your big friend has been seen wandering loose,' Amber reported. 'Distressed, apparently. Will you please have a look for him, before he causes trouble?'

Everything had been fine for a while. Andrew liked the guest house. It was calm and everything about it – the walls, the beams, the furniture – was solid and reliable. A pregnant woman, unrestricted by her size, had shown up and made nice noises at him. Then she got busy sweeping out the rooms and polishing the tables. Andrew just stood there, liking the polish smell as she worked around him.

Andrew was infected by a swarm of tiny but furious creatures. They were lodged in his brain and spinal cord. Right now they were becalmed. The creatures had met in Andrew a host who could not be driven to violence as often as they might like. But they would never stop pushing and they had plenty of influence. Andrew could not remember how they had gotten inside him. He could remember little of his past life. He only caught glimpses of ghosts of warm or cold as they hovered in his peripheral vision. For example, he did not know why he was so happy now. He did not know that the smell of polish was reminding him of home.

The woman polished the television, its glass screen as thick as a ship's porthole. But then, unfortunately, she switched it on.

Andrew jolted, the harmless cabinet was suddenly transformed into an inexplicable box of light and noise. It was crouched into the corner, hissing at him and making him upset. He backed away from it. His infection was awoken.

Another lady arrived carrying a chocolate fudge cake on a round platter. The pregnant lady *ooh*ed and *aah*ed at the cake and said, 'You've excelled yourself again, Gloria.'

'Thank you, Mrs Farr,' said Mrs Melody, taking a playful bow. 'And look, you've brought a lovely shine to the place.'

Gloria Melody cut the cake down the middle then cut one half into three generous slices. She offered the platter up to Andrew but, distracted by the television, he was confused by her gesture. He wanted to behave correctly. He wanted the nice people to like him. He wanted to be normal. But the television was still crackling and spitting at him. Andrew glanced back and forth between the cake and the noise box.

'Have one, you will,' said Mrs Melody. 'Have one, you will. Have one, you will. Have one, you will.'

Assaulted by the woman on one side and the television on the other, Andrew was under pressure. Instead of taking a slice he lifted the other half of the cake, the entire piece. He dropped his jaw open and stuffed the cake down his throat. Surprised, Mrs Melody and the pregnant woman stared for a full five seconds. Then they began to giggle. There was no cruelty in their laughter but they could not stop. 'I love a lad with an appetite,' Mrs Farr gasped, laughing so hard that she almost went into labour.

Andrew looked at the laughing women. He looked at his chocolatey fingers. He knew he had embarrassed himself again. They were laughing at him.

He did not like that.

He growled.

The women stopped laughing and were nervous instead. Andrew knocked them aside as he lurched for the bedrooms. The rest of the cake went flying from Gloria Melody's hand and hit the wall. It clung on a few seconds before beginning a slow slide to the floor.

Andrew could feel the cake's other half sliding down his throat in the same way, clogging his stomach and pumping his bloodstream with sugar. He looked frantically for May or Ewan. They were not there. They had left him alone. He did not like that.

The women scarpered out the door, making anxious noises at one another. The cake had left a wide brown trail down the wall. Andrew stomped over and tried to wipe off the brown stuff but only rubbed it wider. He used more force and ripped a chunk from the plaster. Andrew made a cry – it sounded like a horse's whinny. There was chocolate and dust everywhere. He had made a mess. Everyone would see and everyone would know. He had to get out. He had to get away. He lumbered out of the front door, down the garden path and pushed the gate. It swung open but was spring-loaded so came back at him. He grunted and kicked it. That gate would never swing again.

Andrew did not want people near him. He blundered into the fields. Frustration made his jaw ache. He looked at the cabbages growing around him and felt one would counteract the sickening cake. He snapped a cabbage up and ate it, core and all. It was no comfort. He stomped further, leaving big footprints in the soil.

'Hello.'

A man stepped into Andrew's path. He had a very shiny bald head, sunlight bounced off it and irritated Andrew's eyes. The man's slacks also bothered him. They were a weird anti-crumple material. And luminous yellow.

'Would you like a cup of tea?' Mr Hopkins asked.

Andrew bared his teeth. The man backed off.

Andrew saw the big blue lake. He had an impulse to go there. His brain clanked, the lake must be good because May was always bringing him to it. He lurched passed Mr Hopkins and headed for the jetty. Going through the village Andrew was approached by other people – they were cautious but made nice

58

noises. Andrew lunged about, trying to avoid them. He hated the sun in his eyes. He hated the way his arms swung. He hated the smell of his own breath.

On the jetty the brothers Earlly were settled in deckchairs. They were fishing, using lures they had made themselves of fine thread, duck feathers and steel hooks. Lough Linger did not naturally contain fish. It had been stocked by villagers generations before, releasing fish into it so they would have an extra food supply. Right then, visible through the clear water, fish were approaching the shimmering lures. They swam off as Andrew came stomping down the jetty. The brothers stood, worried, as Andrew bore down on them. The second brother wanted to make a run for it but the first stood firm. 'He *looks* scary,' he said, 'but he's no harm . . . HELLO LAD,' he shouted, as if deafness was Andrew's problem, 'CAN WE HELP YOU?'

The second brother gulped. The monster-boy was only seconds away, his yellow eyes burning. He slumped with relief when Andrew went straight past them and down the steps to the water.

'See?' said the first brother. 'He just wants to take a drink.'

They stepped over to watch.

'The boy is the right age,' said the second brother, and he became eager. 'Do you think he might be taken, right now, before our eyes? All we ever get to see is the arm and hand grabbing out. But if it comes near to the jetty we'll see its whole body! And its face! I'd love to see it all, close up, just once.' He made a pant of excitement. 'I often dream of it.'

The first was disgusted with his younger brother, younger by eleven seconds. 'Those kids are our *guests*,' he said. 'They've nothing to do with our tradition. The boy will drink for a few days, then they'll be sent away. And mind your language, nobody gets *grabbed*.'

'It always looks like a grab to me,' said the second, stung by his brother's criticism. 'It moves fast. And takes a tight hold.'

'Our guardian is gentle,' said the first, 'he . . . excuse me, *it* does not grab.'

'And I'd love to see, once and for all, if it's male or female,' said the second. 'I don't like saying *it*. Things were simpler when we were boys. He was a *he* and that was that. You knew where you stood.'

'I have no objection to saying *it*,' said the first brother. 'I'm moving with the times. The ladies were right, we never had any reason to assume our guardian was male. And we don't need to know either way. Let it have its privacy.'

They looked down at the monster-boy again. There was no movement in the water around him. He was making crude animal noises as he licked at the lake.

'The Founder knows what kind of person our guardian will want,' said the first brother. 'And, bless him, the likes of this boy would never get approval.'

60

Andrew was trying to lap up water. Again it fizzed in his throat and refused to go down. He scooped some in his hand. He watched while the pool in his palm turned distinctly grey and bubbles began popping against his skin. Andrew flung the tainted water away and whimpered. Why did the lake hate him? Because . . .

Monster = Bad.

Lough Linger's surface remained impassive. It held its secrets. Andrew was like a pilgrim who walked a thousand kilometres only to find the temple closed to him. If the lake had been a door Andrew would have pounded on it. But it was not. It was a blue plate of cool perfection. The absolute opposite of him, the angry, sweaty beast.

Me = Monster.

Andrew flopped on the bottom step, bowed his head and cried. His tears were yellow and full of bony grit. They splashed into the lake but even they would not be accepted by the crystal-bright waters. Andrew's tears sank away but Lough Linger did not mix with them.

7

Mr Merriman drank a pint of lake water. It was the first thing he did every morning. He felt its invigorating properties trickle down to his toes. The second thing Mr Merriman did every morning was write a list on a piece of paper. This was his day's itinerary. All fine solid tasks that he would enjoy ticking off. He liked making lists. He liked having a plan. Right then Mr Merriman had a flash of inspiration. He turned the page over and wrote on the back, *Mrs Merriman, it is my plan* . . .' That was all he could think of for the moment. It was a good start though, simple and true.

It would be the opening line of a love poem he wanted to compose to his wife. It was their anniversary soon and they had been married a very long time. He would strive to make the poem excellent. He had heard on the radio that many poets did not care for rhyme these days. But, to Mr Merriman, a poem had to be made to rhyme. Anything else was plain lazy.

First item on the list: write to seed suppliers. He had no requirements this month but had something to return. In his last order the suppliers had accidentally sent him two extra packets of sunflower seeds. He put them in an envelope to post back later and included a cheery note. Mr Merriman was nothing if not honest.

Mrs Merriman, it is my plan / to remain your true man.

He turned the rhyme over in his mouth a few times. Not bad. But he believed he could do better.

Second item on the list: chop firewood. Most men Mr Merriman's age would not even be able to lift his long-handled axe. But most men did not have the benefit of drinking from Lough Linger. Each log was halved cleanly, at the rate of four a minute. To the rhythm of chopping, Mr Merriman sought the poem's next phrase. It was tricky to write poetry when you had not read much poetry. Mr Merriman did not read books of any sort. Generally, he only read seed packets. Reading a book could never be as rewarding as simply feeling the sun on your eyelids or admiring the stars, so why do it? He thought reading was for people who were dissatisfied, people who felt they were missing out. He knew that Mr Swift, the school teacher, loved reading and, yes, that fitted. He had never gotten over losing the girl he loved in his youth. Now Mr Swift took long walks alone and was often seen looking up towards where the paths left the valley. Reading had not helped him. Eunice Boswell liked the *Reader's Digest* but that was probably harmless. Mr Swift liked big books with no pictures and small print. He had even expressed the desire to *write* a book. Imagine! Needing to read them was one thing but needing to write them too. To be so troubled by the world that you had to invent a new one.

Mr Merriman leaned on his axe and looked out over the lake. He was happy in this place. He needed no other. Mr Merriman was nothing if not content.

Mrs Merriman, it is my plan / to stay here; who needs Japan?

Maybe. But he did not want to trouble Mrs Merriman with the idea that her husband had been contemplating Asia.

Third item on the list: turn soil in carrot patch. He went for his spade and discovered that Mrs Merriman had covered its rough wooden grip with a swatch of material and glued it in place. There was no danger of getting a splinter now. He felt a surge of appreciation for his wife. Mr Merriman was nothing if not grateful.

Mrs Merriman, it is my plan / to be your number one fan.

Nice, but not quite right.

Mr Merriman inched along, slicing in and turning the soil methodically. He had a big carrot patch so this was a big job. He put the poem to the back of his mind. He would return to it some other day, the gardening was more important right now.

Mr Merriman was nothing if not focused.

But that was unfortunate. Writing a love poem to his wife was the best thing he could have done that day. Everything else was going to be wasted. He would never post that letter. He would never burn that firewood. He would never taste those carrots. In a few days Mr Merriman and Mrs Merriman would both die.

Mr Merriman felt a rumble. He stopped – was it his heart? Was this the end? No, the tremor was coming up through his knees. He felt it again. Was something digging under there? He looked around but there was only the village and the peaceful lake. Mr Merriman dared to hope, *a Lesser-Spotted Blossom?* Could one have taken root in his carrot patch and be about to burst out? 'How wonderful that would be,' Mr Merriman said aloud. He scurried back to his shed. You did not want to get in this blossom's way. He watched the earth excitedly. To have a Lesser-Spotted Blossom grow in one's own garden! There was no better omen.

The two brothers were fishing from the jetty when Andrew, May and Ewan walked to school and were still there when they came back. They seemed to spend all day every day on the jetty and had not even begun to paint the rowboat.

'It is curious,' admitted Ewan.

'Completely wacko, is what it is,' said May. 'I bet it's something to do with us. They started fishing when we arrived and haven't stopped since.'

'Perhaps it's for Andrew's meals.'

'Andrew eats a lot but he isn't getting a tonne of fish for his dinners.'

'I am sure the explanation is something harmless,' said Ewan, 'and probably something . . . nice.'

May just rolled her eyes.

'If you'd prefer,' said Ewan, 'we can take Andrew elsewhere for his afternoon drink.'

'Aye,' said May, 'follow me.'

They continued through the village and out the other side, seeking somewhere more private. Lough Linger's shore had no sandy beaches or muddy banks, that would be too much like untidiness. It was clean-edged rock slabs and boulders all the way around. They found a quiet spot not too far from the village. They stepped off the path and over the tops of a dozen boulders to get to it. At the shore were two enormous rocks, the size of cottages. Between them was a snug inlet. Today Andrew needed a lot of persuasion to drink from the lake. May had to shove him to the rim and spend minutes encouraging him to take a gulp. He tried hard, wanting to please her, but it was like drinking ants. He spat and saw that the water had gone from crystal clear to pasty grey in his mouth. He looked back to May and Ewan but they were too busy making noises at each other to notice his problem. Meekly, he tried again.

May and Ewan clambered to the top of one the massive rocks. 'I love the school here,' Ewan was saying. 'Mr Swift is brilliant.'

'I don't like the way he's always eyeing up Andrew,' said May. She lay back on the boulder and closed her eyes, cushioning her head in her hands and letting the sun warm her.

'Andrew *is* sort of interesting-looking,' said Ewan reasonably. 'Besides, Andrew doesn't mind. I think he likes the attention.'

'It's ye who likes attention,' said May.

Ewan let that one slide. He looked out over the glassy surface of Lough Linger and was reminded of the community centre window. That giant hand reaching out. 'What lives in the lake?' he asked.

. . . move . . . still . . . move . . . nibble . . . mmmm . . . move. . .

'Just fish,' said May, with her eyes closed.

'What kind of fish?' asked Ewan.

'The big kind.'

Ewan shaded his eyes and watched the distant shapes on the jetty. One of the brothers Earlly was reeling in a fish at that moment. He needed both arms to hold the fish to his chest as it bucked against him. The fish was so large it appeared unreal. It could feed a family for a fortnight. But it was still just a fish, nothing unusual. Nothing that might have a giant arm.

'Is there anything . . .' Ewan asked slowly, 'bigger?'

'Monsters on the brain,' said May, without opening her eyes.

Ewan looked at the lake a while more. May kept her face to the sky.

'The *people* are the freaky thing around here,' said May. 'Everyone in that school lives with both their parents. That's not *so* weird. But all their grandparents are still alive *and* all their great-grandparents.'

'It is exceptional,' admitted Ewan. He had even heard mention of great-great-grandparents still alive and well but did not mention that now.

'I've ever seen nor heard of so many old people in me life,' said May.

'Being old is no crime,' said Ewan. 'Besides, it makes sense that there're more old people here than in the average village. The waters give health and long life. Think about it, the proportion of old people is bound to get higher all the time.'

Ewan stuck his hand down his collar and felt his upper back. His spots had disappeared. He looked at his nails, they were even and hard, like ceramic. He shook his head and felt his hair bounce. 'I'm starting to notice the effect myself,' he said.

Andrew was done trying to drink. His bones clanged as he got to his feet. May's boredom fell away, and she rose on her elbows and looked at him. No sign of the change she longed for. Andrew was still locked away in his monster body. She sank back down and closed her eyes again, blinking the world away.

'The water's made no difference to Andrew,' she said.

'Perhaps Andrew's infection is too deep,' said Ewan. He saw May curl up in reaction, as if his words had caused her physical pain, and he felt bad. 'I'm sorry, May, I really am,' he said, 'but you have to face the possibility that Andrew might be stuck like this for life.'

'No I don't,' said May. 'Never.'

A boy and a girl were walking down the path from the village. When the boy saw the visitors he dashed ahead and vaulted over the boulders towards them. It was Tim, wanting another look at the monster-boy. But it was unwise to approach Andrew so rapidly and directly. Andrew's instincts flared and he spun at the boy and snarled.

'Whoooa,' said the boy. He dug in his heels, leaving rubber streaks on the granite. 'You should keep him leashed.'

May sprang up and glared at Tim. 'Ye better have some manners,' she warned him. 'Andrew could twist your head open and have your brains for chewing gum.'

Tim's light-stepping companion arrived. She put her hands on his shoulders in a sisterly manner. She smelled of vanilla. It was the mysterious girl from the classroom. Ewan stood up and ran his fingers through his hair.

'Hello,' he said.

'Please forgive Tim's rudeness,' the girl said, her voice a sugary whisper. 'He and I are used to doing what we want. We're the Brides of the Lake.'

Ewan glanced at Tim.

'Yeah, yeah,' he said, 'the boys get called Brides too, get over it.'

'Brides, grooms, whatever,' said May, 'it won't matter to Andrew when he's wiping his nose on your brain tissue.'

'You shouldn't talk nasty like that in front of Brigit and me,' Tim said to her.

'*Sorrieeee,*' said May.

To May's horror, Brigit gazed at her openly, put her hand over her heart, did her holy icon impression, and whispered, 'I forgive you.'

In Lough Linger they did not know cruelty, spite, sour milk, bad weather or, it seemed, sarcasm. 'I don't want forgiveness from ye,' May had to explain.

'I have already given it,' said Brigit.

'Well, take it back,' said May.

'We each have the power to forgive,' said Brigit.

70

'You cannot opt in or out of another's forgiving. I accept that you do not want it. Nonetheless, I have given it. Please try to accept that.'

'You're *sooo* convinced of yourself but really you're just afraid of the rough aul world,' said May. 'By being able to forgive everything ye reckon nothing can touch ye, 'cos ye are *above* everything. Maybe ye are. But I'd rather be down here and fighting for what's right. Even if it hurts sometimes.'

Ewan watched Brigit for her reaction. It was impossible to tell if May's words had any effect. Ewan found their clash interesting. May was narky and unpredictable. Brigit was smooth and consistent. They were both dominating personalities in their different ways. May's strength was in pushing all the time. Brigit's came from staying soft as cream.

Eventually Brigit said, 'There is no hurt in Lough Linger.'

May just snorted but Ewan felt the words slide comfortably home. Like a warm towel folded away. Like sitting by a fire on a stormy night. A place without hurt was the place to be. Being near to Brigit would be nice too. Ewan blinked and looked away. He realised that he was staring at her.

May sat, then stretched out on the boulder. She closed her eyes, as if these two sheltered wimps, Brigit and Tim, were so boring it was physically impossible for her to stay awake.

'What does it mean, to be a Bride of the Lake?' Ewan asked them.

'It means . . .' Brigit and Tim looked at each other. 'It means we get to live with our Uncle someday. Just like we've always wanted.'

'Oh,' said Ewan. He was expecting something more dramatic.

'There you are!' someone shouted from the path. It was Mr Swift, waving his cane. 'Come quick and bring Andrew,' he called. 'A Lesser-Spotted Blossom has sprouted. This is an exciting day.'

8

Everything was shared in Lough Linger, including excitement. Everyone had shared in the excitement when Mr Hume finally got his philosophy degree from the Open University. They raised him on their shoulders and paraded him around the village. Everyone shared in the excitement when Mr Wright's wheaten loaf recipe came second in a national competition. He won a medal and got to meet a famous chef from the television. The entire village took the afternoon off to hear about it. Everyone shared in the excitement when the Honeyfords had a posh new toilet fitted. They took turns using it.

So everyone soon knew about the plant's appearance. Villagers stood from their work and called to each other across the fields. 'A Lesser-Spotted Blossom has appeared.' 'Where?' 'In the Merrimans' garden.' 'How wonderful!'

They dropped what they were doing and hurried to the site of the sprouting, gathering up neighbours as they went. Word reached Carrick McCuddy as he polished his blood donation medals. Carrick gave blood regularly. To do so he went to the big city three times a year. This, everyone agreed, made him a fine, brave man. That he donated blood there too made the whole thing even more impressive. Now he put down his medals and rose from his armchair, eager to see the blossom. Word reached Gloria Melody, and she hummed a happy tune as she headed for the Merrimans' cottage. Word reached Mrs Bird's salon. She abandoned a hairdo midway and scuttled out. Her customers went too. Every citizen of Lough Linger was on their way. Andrew stomped along in the middle of the crowd, head and shoulders above everyone else.

'It's a plant of some sort,' Mr Swift explained to the visitors as they walked. 'It grows only in our valley but not often, even here. All the properties of the lake are concentrated strongly in a Lesser-Spotted Blossom. But the plant always retracts back into the ground after a few hours. We must be quick.'

Mr Merriman was beaming and welcoming everybody. People shook his hand and congratulated him. Hosting a sprouting always brought good luck. Once a Lesser-Spotted Blossom had burst straight through the Fosters' living room floor. A month later Mr Foster won six prizes in a market garden competition and Mrs Foster was pregnant with twins.

A mound of earth had been coughed up and carrots pushed up early. The Lesser-Spotted Blossom had burst from the peak and was wobbling in the breeze. Ewan had spent countless hours watching natural history documentaries but had never seen anything like this. Not on the BBC and not on Channel 4, not in any National Geographic box set and not in the DVD extras. The sprouting was taller than a person. Not much like a blossoming flower, it was more like the cross between a cactus and a jellyfish. Mostly it was a gelatinous alien, hardly belonging to this world at all. It was faintly luminescent, as if had it been night instead of day the plant might have been seen to glow. A milky translucent trunk tapered up out of the ground. It would have been waxy to the touch and springy like rubber. Ribs of harder flesh ran from root to tip and kept the plant vertical. Stubby growths, like fat thumbs, were sticking out from the ribs and wibbling and wobbling. The whole Lesser-Spotted Blossom quivered, shifting its weight this way and that but just solid enough to keep from flopping over. Its skin shimmered with a strange paste that poured off and over itself constantly like wax melting and solidifying again. It was this that the people of Lough Linger craved. Men, women and children all formed queues to drink from the plant. There was no pushing or shoving. They supported each other, leaning tight together in a scrum, and nibbled at its oozing surface.

Everyone gave the plant a few solid licks before stepping back and allowing someone else a turn.

'Wonderful,' said Carrick McCuddy, shaking out his old legs. 'I can feel it taking years off me.'

'It's absolutely gorgeous,' agreed Mrs Foster, licking her lips.

'A particularly fine aroma,' said Mr Hopkins. He leaned over and his wife rubbed some of the wax into his bald scalp. It gave it a nice shine.

'There's great goodness in it,' said Mr Hume as he picked some stringy matter from his beard.

May and Ewan looked at each other. The villagers were like a litter of piglets suckling on a fat sow.

'That . . .' said May with slow certainty, 'is gross.'

Mr Swift raised his cane, handle in palm, and it swung like a pendulum. He was considering how this scene might appear to the outsiders. 'We believe it is worth the benefits,' he said at last. 'We believe anything is.'

'How can those things just burst up then disappear?' Ewan asked. 'Aren't there roots you can dig down to?'

'Too deep,' said Farmer Able. 'I reckon they grow all the way from under the lake. I wudnae try ta take a cutting, either. Goes back under like greased lightning if you try to grab a cutting offa one.'

'Andrew, I think you should drink from it,' said Mr Swift, turning to the monster-boy.

A doubtful growl was turning in Andrew's throat. The plant had his instincts tingling. He felt another tickle and looked down. May had taken him by the hand. She looked into his eyes and made reassuring noises. Andrew allowed himself to be led forwards. Villagers stepped aside. The monster-boy could skip the queue, he was their guest and, besides, his need was greatest. The plant smelled of the deep dank earth. Its sway made Andrew anxious. Instinct told him not to drink from it at all, but to tear the thing down and stomp it into chunks. The nodules on the plant's ribs began to wobble faster. Andrew recoiled. He dragged May back with him. He looked over his shoulder, seeking reassurance. But the villagers shiny smiles only made him feel worse. One face comforted him. It was Mr Swift's, looking serious. They locked eyes and were for a moment connected. Mr Swift made a slight nod.

Andrew turned back to the Lesser-Spotted Blossom. Shyly, he poked out his tongue. It was an ugly tongue, like a slab of raw beef, and Andrew did not like people seeing it. He leaned forward, and the plant jumped.

It did not jump out of the ground, rather it jolted and swung from him. Villagers yelped. Some had to dodge away to avoid being struck by it. Andrew stepped after the plant. Carrots snapped under his feet. It seemed frightened of the monster-boy, its thumb-like protuberances jiggling in organic panic. Again the sprouting danced away from him. Now this had become a chase and Andrew's infection began to boil. His fingers hardened into grappling hooks. He lunged after the plant. Again it swung away. The Lesser-Spotted Blossom was much more than swaying, it was shifting dramatically. The circle of villagers pulled back, getting wider and wider as Andrew lunged after the plant, going around and around.

He would never win this way. Andrew stopped and studied the plant through narrow eyes. It halted too. It seemed to be waiting. Andrew's brain, normally clogged and slow, was sharp when battle tactics were required. He looked to where the plant disappeared into the ground. The upper plant could swing plenty but its base was held by the hole it had sprouted from.

Andrew dropped, slammed his knees into the soil and wrapped his hands around the lower truck. He aimed his open jaws at the plant, not caring anymore what people thought of his tongue. It startled even May and Ewan to see just how wide Andrew could extend his mouth; it was a yellow-toothed bear-trap.

The ground trembled.

Andrew hesitated, his mouth hanging open. With startling speed the Lesser-Spotted Blossom withdrew into the ground, slipping sloppily through Andrew's hands and leaving him grasping the air. A shake and a slurp and the plant was gone.

The villagers glanced at each other. It had been the briefest blossoming anyone could remember.

'Oooh,' said Mr Wright to his wife sadly, 'I didn't get a lick in.' Both the Wrights had chubby pink faces. Right now their faces were chubby, pink and unhappy.

Andrew looked around. His grunt sounded like a question.

The villagers were disappointed. Mr Wright was not the only one, most had not gotten a taste of the blossom, but they were too mannerly to blame their guests.

'Another will pop up in a few months, probably,' said Carrick.

'Indeed,' said Mr Farr. He was the owner of the sawmill and always had sawdust in his thick black hair. 'Sometimes unfortunate things happen, but life goes on.'

Yes, everyone agreed. The villagers cheered up. There would be plenty more chances. Life was long.

'I've just made a batch of scones,' said Mrs Grace.

'And I'll make a big pot of tea,' said Mr Hopkins.

9

Ewan followed the path Brigit and Tim were on when they had met. Soon he was past that spot and in unexplored territory. Up ahead, above the lake in a plantation, Ewan saw the top of a stone tower peeking above the pines. The tower was just crooked enough to look like a fairy tale. *That place would suit Brigit*, thought Ewan. Just as he thought it, her pale face materialised at the highest window. She gazed at the lake then withdrew.

Ewan looked at the clumps of flowers growing by the path. Their colourful petals rose and fell like wisps on the breeze. Plump bumblebees were busy pollinating. Ewan looked right and left then reached out and tugged a flower out of the ground. Clingy perfume spilled from it. Ewan picked another flower, and another. This was shaping up to be a bunch.

An apple descended from the branches above. It hovered before Ewan's face. The apple was in a hand on the end of Amber Feather's arm. Ewan looked up and saw that she was stretched out in the branches of the apple tree. 'Have one,' she said, 'it's organic.'

The Mayor had been resting her eyes on the lake, taking a break from her daily responsibilities. Not that her job was tough. Mostly it was patting children's heads with one hand while dispensing favours with the other. Arranging community events was easy when everyone was so co-operative. Making sure everyone had enough was easy when you lived in this valley of plenty. Amber was in love with her work.

Ewan controlled his surprise at seeing her. 'Thank you,' he said, accepting the fruit with one hand and hiding the flowers behind his back with the other.

'Where are you going?' asked Amber.

'Oh, nowhere,' said Ewan, looking back and forth along the path. He dropped the flowers.

Amber looked in the tower's direction, its top visible above the pines. The tower was, as towers tended to be, a highly obvious destination. She smiled, then wound her way out of the tree, coiling herself around the trunk as she descended.

'Are you enjoying your time in our valley?' she asked.

'Yes, everyone is so good to us.' Ewan spoke slowly, watching the Mayor. He was not yet sure if she was a *stay-as-long-as-you-like* host, like Mr Swift. Or more of an *isn't-it-time-you-were-going*, like Miss

Boswell. Which type Amber was could be important. She was Mayor, after all.

'Good to know,' said Amber, not giving anything away. 'I was born here so I'm biased but I doubt there's a finer place in the world. I'm also sure there's no better job than to be Mayor of Lough Linger. I'll run for election again when my term's up.'

'I am sorry Andrew scared away the blossom,' said Ewan.

'Another will grow some day,' said Amber. 'Don't worry about it.'

'And he's broken the guest house gate,' said Ewan. 'I apologise for that too.'

Amber smiled. She saw Ewan was about to say more but stopped himself. 'Anything else?' she asked playfully.

'May broke a window and smashed a plate and Andrew keeps wandering into fields and eating people's cabbages. I am sorry. He's hard to stop when he wants something. I hope you won't think we're hooligans. Or at least . . .' and here Ewan got to his real worry, 'you won't think *I* am one.'

Amber laughed. 'I certainly don't. But tell me, Ewan, what does it matter what I think?'

Ewan was nervous. He began slowly, 'I would like if . . . whatever happens with Andrew and May . . . you'd consider letting me stay here in Lough Linger.'

'Oh,' said Amber, and her features went soft.

'I don't mean forever,' Ewan rushed to add. 'I've no parents but in a couple of years I'll be old enough to do what I want. Until then Social Services will want to keep me in some horrible institution. I just need somewhere to be for a while.'

'Your situation is difficult for me to imagine,' said Amber. 'No one is ever orphaned in Lough Linger.'

'I am not an orphan,' said Ewan, 'my father's alive, but in prison.'

Amber Feather sighed at the brutality of it all. No one in Lough Linger ever went to prison, either. Then, to Ewan's surprise, she took a step forwards and seized Ewan in a hug. Her golden hair fell about him. The hug happened too quickly for Ewan to be embarrassed. He stood locked against her until she released him and stepped back.

Ewan was dazed. 'I'd vote for you,' he said.

Amber grinned. 'We don't really vote in Lough Linger,' she explained. 'In our elections we just have tea and chat about things until we all agree. Which is what we'll have to do if you want to stay longer. Let's see what Fredrick says first. He's our grandest citizen, but don't worry, it'll just be a chat. Just be yourself.'

Amber led Ewan along the path, away from the tower and further from the village. Swallows were skimming the lake surface. Newts sat on rocks and tasted the air. In a while they were approaching a lonely stone building. Grass grew from its roof. It was close to the lake edge and Ewan remembered villagers saying that in the future more people would get to drink from Lough Linger.

'Miss Feather?' began Ewan.

'Please, call me Amber.'

'Amber, is the lake rising?' he asked.

'Well observed,' she said. 'It *is* rising, slowly, every year. We'll have to take this house down soon and rebuild it on higher ground.'

'There aren't any rivers flowing in,' said Ewan, 'there must be a spring underneath that feeds it.'

'The story goes that when Fredrick Fredricksson first found these waters it was just a pond,' said Amber. 'So, as you can see, it's expanded a lot. Fredricksson was so in love with these waters that he never left its shore again. He claims to be able to talk to the lake, if you can believe that. He was the first citizen of this valley. Everyone you have met here is a descendant of one of the planters who followed him. He isn't called Fredricksson much anymore. We just call him the Founder.'

Stunned, Ewan stopped. They were by the house. Lough Linger was a large lake – if it was a pond when the Founder discovered it, then that must have been many generations ago. 'The original Founder is still alive?' he asked.

'I think you've noticed that our lives are long here,'

said Amber. 'But the Founder's has been longest of all.'

What kind of lake can do this? wondered Ewan. 'Amber,' he asked, 'is anything unusual living in the lake?'

'No,' she said, 'nothing unusual.'

Amber opened the door. The building was all one dull chamber with a tiny yellow window. It smelled of damp cardboard. There were strange knobbly sculptures in the corners and stuck to the ceilings, difficult to make out in the semi-darkness. Old books were overloading bent shelves. A four-poster bed took up most of the room. Drapes hung from its posts – they looked once-upon-a-time luxurious, like the curtains of an abandoned theatre. The blankets appeared leaden, hanging off the bed and slumping weightily on the floor. In bed, with books scattered around him, a man lay on his back. The Founder was small but his breathing was big. It was a deep gurgle, as if his throat was a sinkhole plunging underground. He was so pale he almost glowed. Each side of his face, his fingers held the edge of a blanket to his chin. The fingers moved non-stop, rising and falling as if they were the feelers on a sea anemone waving in an ocean current. He was looking straight at Ewan.

'Why have you brought him here?' the Founder asked Amber. His voice was watery and trembling. He was like some rare and helpless creature suddenly caught in the lights of a camera crew. Rooted to the spot, frightened of getting attacked, but unable to move or even look away.

'This is not the monster-boy,' said Amber. 'This is his friend. He's a smart lad. I'd like you to meet him.'

The Founder's breathing was the only sound for a while. His fear faded. Then he said, 'Please . . . come here so I can see you.'

The carpet sank and popped under Ewan's step. It was strange, like walking on bubble wrap. The Founder was no longer frightened and lowered the blanket from his chin. He was chubby, hairless and helpless like a baby. Ewan was certain he never got out of bed. Perhaps he never even rolled over. But despite the Founder's helplessness there was always that loud breathing, gusty and wet, like wind and rain blowing through a cave.

'Handsome fellow,' said the Founder.

Ewan wanted to make a clever reply but could not think of anything in time. So he just held his hands together and stood there. His eyes adjusted to the dark chamber. It was then Ewan noticed that all the books were black with mould. It was kind of repulsive. Then Ewan noticed that the knobbly sculptures around the room were not sculptures at all. They were clumps of brown mushrooms growing out of the damp floor, walls and ceiling. Dozens of them, some the size of dinner plates. The Founder's blankets were heavy because they were supporting layers of mould, inches thick, green and hairy. Ewan knew the phrase 'made your skin crawl' but had never lived it until now. His skin lurched and writhed, it might have crawled right off his body. The Founder stank of stagnation, the carpet was a fungus farm and the air was dense with a billion breeding microbes.

The Founder was looking Ewan over, appraising him with his wet eyes. It was a struggle not to scream and run. How could anybody live like this? Yet it seemed the Founder was well-respected. He obviously wanted a home like a swamp. His tongue ran once over his lips before slipping back in.

'Have you ever read *Oliver Twist*?' the Founder asked Ewan, referring to the mouldy book lying open on the bed.

'No,' said Ewan, too quickly. Then he added, 'I saw a version on television.' Ewan was glad to be talking, anything to distract him from this nightmarish room.

The Founder did not seem disappointed. 'A marvellous story, whichever way one consumes it,' he said.

'I do read books,' said Ewan, 'but I prefer fact to fiction.'

'Fiction can contain truths, can it not?' said the Founder. 'Important truths are sometimes beyond the reach of science or history.' His voice was deep but edgeless and warbling, like a gargle. Ewan realised that the Founder had no teeth.

'Perhaps you are right, Mr Founder, fiction writers have witnessed things that they want to put in their stories. But then why dress them up?'

'For our delight,' suggested the Founder. He made a gummy smile. He was enjoying this mild and respectful argument. '*Oliver Twist* has such a charming ending. It gives me more pleasure every time I read it.'

'I don't usually like happy endings,' said Ewan. 'I'd like to but . . . I don't trust them. Life's never been like that for me.'

'Let me assure you,' said the Founder, 'all endings are happy in Lough Linger.'

'I hope so,' said Ewan.

'Is your soul good?' the Founder asked him.

Ewan had no answer for that. He shuffled on his feet. Puffball mushrooms burst beneath his shoes.

'Untainted?' the Founder asked.

'I don't know,' said Ewan. 'I've done some bad things but some good things too. I am learning, I hope.'

'I admire your honesty,' said the Founder. 'Honesty is important for one's soul.'

The Founder offered his hand. Ewan's stomach turned. All he could see were blue veins beneath sickly skin.

Ewan was the sort of boy who enjoyed shaking hands. He thought it was a sign of uprightness.

Reliable people shook hands, admirable people shook hands. The kind of people that people looked up to. But now he held his breath as he reached out.

The Founder's hand was bloated and squishy, like a rubber glove full of water.

It was a long five seconds before the Founder let go of him. Ewan breathed again. The Founder's eyelids slid back over his eyes, pressing out moisture that rolled down his cheeks. He lowered his head into the ancient dent in his pillow and exhaled.

'You have my approval,' said the Founder.

Amber ushered Ewan to the door. It was relief to be out of that fungus factory. Amber was obviously relieved too. 'There now,' she said, breathing in the fresh air. She gave Ewan a smile and said, 'I had a feeling he'd like you.'

10

May climbed to where she had met Theodora. The wind turbines were turning in the distance, barely visible through shrouds of rain. The same wind that turned them was whipping rain squalls inside the valley's invisible borders. They wet the hilltop but got no further. May hung around for an hour, watching the villagers mowing their lawns and sheep mowing their fields.

Bored, May hiked down and up again to the next hilltop. She came across strange rock formations. They were like stumpy tree trunks but of stone not wood. They were attached to the hillside, formed from the same granite. Some of them had their tops knocked off but most were taller than May. There were nine of the strange pillars in a row. They were worth taking a photograph of but May did not have a camera. Soon bored of the formations, she moved on to the next hill, and the next. It was Theodora that May longed to see. But Theodora did not appear.

She descended back into the valley, through pine plantations, past the sawmill and out onto farmland.

. . . *WeChewGrass* . . . *WeChewGrass* . . . *WeChewGrass* . . .

The sheep were around their owner, Farmer Able. While his flock munched he was just standing there and staring at the empty air, the way old people are often content to do. His woolly hat was pulled down and he was leaning heavily on his walking stick. The stick was the dark knobbly kind that old farmers always preferred. Mr Swift used his cane for display and theatrics but Farmer Able actually needed his stick to hold him up.

'I coulda used a wee sup of that sprouting,' he said to May. 'But your pal spooked it before I got the chance.'

'*Sorrieee*,' said May.

'Oh no,' said Farmer Able, embarrassed. 'No need to apologise, I was only saying.'

May did not bother to argue. The sun was going down and she headed for the guest house. Ewan had just returned, carrying the dinners a neighbour had made for them. He and Andrew were both having fish pie. Ewan's was served in a stoneware dish. Andrew's was in a steel bucket filled to the brim. May was having spinach pie – she was a vegetarian. It warmed Ewan to see that everyone's appetites were known and catered for by the village. He put the bucket down in front of Andrew and gave him his favourite wooden spoon. Andrew did not wait for anyone else to start, he got chomping. It was dark now and Ewan switched on a few lights. Rather than the overhead he used the table lamps – they were cosier. Everything was so comfortable in this house, in this whole valley. Only one thing disturbed Ewan: the Founder.

'He was the most horrible person I've ever seen,' Ewan told May over dinner. 'But still, he's not typical of people here, is he?' He took a sip from his glass of water.

May was not really listening to him. She was tuned into something else, something beyond Ewan's senses.

'A visitor is walking through the village,' she said. 'The dogs can smell the outside world on their clothes.'

'Perhaps the girl you met has decided to come home?' suggested Ewan. May had told him a little about Theodora.

'Doubt it,' said May, 'I think Theodora was just taking a last look. She didn't trust this place. I don't blame her.'

Andrew burped, causing the lampshades to shake. He scraped the bottom of the bucket with his wooden spoon.

'Do you think Lough Linger is really so suspicious?' Ewan asked May. 'Or is it just us?'

'What do ye mean?'

'Everybody here is happy. They all look out for

each other and don't have any anger at anything. Yet, we find that *weird*. We think there's got to be something wrong with them. But perhaps they've got it right. Perhaps they're the strong ones. It's just that we're so unfamiliar with happiness that we don't even recognise it.'

May swallowed some pie. 'Nah,' she said. 'This place stinks.'

There was a knock on the door. Andrew pulled his head from the bucket and stared at the source of the noise. May jumped to her feet, maybe it was Theodora after all. But when May opened the door she found someone else there, someone completely unexpected. She went cold. It was her dad.

'May ...' he said. He reached out to her but faltered, already lost for words.

May reeled away as if he was radioactive. 'What do ye want?' she demanded.

'To take you home,' he said.

'Home?' she said. 'Are ye joking? How'd ye find this place?'

'Your grandmother ... my mother,' he said. 'She read my palm and told me where to look.'

May began to shake. A kind of hardening climbed, in fits and starts, up her spine and into her jaw. Pure rage congealed inside her.

May Unhappy = Bad.

Andrew did not like that. His knees unfolded and

he rose. May's father was outside the door and had no idea of the danger he was in. Ewan leaped onto Andrew's shoulders, he tried to hold him down but it was useless. Ewan's feet left the ground.

'May!' called Ewan, drawing her attention to the situation.

May turned. '*Andrew!*' she snapped. 'Sit DOWN.'

Just like that, he sat.

May pushed out past her dad and strode away. She had changed a lot since he had last seen her. She stood straight, she walked tall. Her dad doddered down the path behind her.

'May,' he said, 'you're too young to be out in the world.'

'Been out in the world since I was two. Go away! You're history!'

'Come home,' he pleaded. 'I've quit the drink and got us a house. You'll like it. It has a garden, I put up bird tables—'

'Is that what ye think is goin' to happen?' May spun and scoffed at him. 'We're goin' to play house?'

He was looking at her with his needy eyes. May felt her guts wrapping tight inside her. She became knotted with anger, bending over and clutching at her own cheeks. 'Go away. GO AWAY,' she blared like a siren. Half the village could hear May's tantrum but were too respectful to peek out of their windows.

'GO AWAY. GO AWAY.'

Those needy eyes. May could not stand them. She turned her back and stared across the lake's black water. She was panting hard, this much hatred was exhausting. Somewhere out in the dark swans were awakening, uncurling their necks and stretching their wings.

'May, please talk to me. Please?'

'Go away.'

GoAwayGoAway . . .

May's childhood had been huddled and painful. Her dad's cowardice was to blame. The worst thing was this – he had let her believe it was normal, normal to be frightened and ashamed all of the time. No. Never again. Since escaping him and leaving her hometown, May had grown into her amazing power. She had faced evil and survived. She did not need her dad. On the contrary, she had to stay away from him. He was toxic to her. She would accept no normal life, no sheep's life, no ordinary life.

'May. Please?'

Her reply came in the form of a blare of loud honks from over the water. The cacophony was slightly comic, like a troupe of clowns squeezing their noses. But the honks were angry too. And getting closer. Then came the stiff sounds of air pressed into work. Something swooped out of the darkness. A flash of white and a flap of wind cut low over May's dad. He ducked.

'May?'

The bird was gone but had left something behind that drifted towards the ground. It passed close to his face. He could not take his eyes off it. A single white feather.

GoAWAY . . . GoAWAY . . .

Other swans were dragging themselves off the lake. When at rest, bellies bowled in the water, the swans could not fully flap their wings. So they kicked their flat feet onto the surface and jogged into take-off. They launched. Their wings broke into two-metre spans, thudding the air as they locked into position. Their necks slung between their shoulders seemed to drag their bulbous bodies behind them. They turned in formation and aimed for the village. Swans are elegant but strong. These were big, hard-boned, mechanised meat with a fat fuselage. Their wings were beaters. Their beaks were stabbers. Many living things feared them. If a dozen adult swans were flying at you then you would fear them too.

May's dad took a hit. The creature ploughed into him, honked in his ear then spun away, shedding feathers and lake water. Pulling himself up he was slammed over by another swan. He cried to May but she kept her back to him. She made no sign of knowing or caring what was happening.

GOAWAYGOAWAY

A swan barrelled out of the night, retracting its neck

and wings in time to make itself a ball. It struck May's dad, bowling him off the ground. The swan rolled away on the air, its wings re-extended and it flapped away on massive, slow, beats.

'MAAAY.'

He was hit again and again, thrown right and left. He staggered back up the path, covering his head with one arm and swinging blindly with the other. The onslaught continued. The swans swooped in, smothering him and jostling him onwards, in an assault of honks, knocks and turbulence.

'I'm going, I'm going,' he pleaded. He did not stop running until he was out of the valley.

Not once did May look over her shoulder. The swans had acted on her impulse, doing what she wanted. It was exhilarating but frightening. May was disturbed by the depth of her own rage, it felt bottom-less. It was like standing on the edge of shadowy pit, not being able to see down but sensing that it dropped many kilometres. All the way to the earth's bubbling core.

11

Ewan and Andrew sat alone in class for the next couple of days. Mr Swift and the students were too diplomatic to ask questions about May's absence. One of the Honeyford boys had lent Ewan a white shirt with bleached cuffs and he was wearing it. Andrew passed the time with his eyes closed, enjoying the pleasant noises everyone made in response to the teacher's pleasant noises.

At the front of the class Brigit seldom spoke. Between the heads of other students Ewan could see the flowers in her hair.

It was break time. Ewan sipped lake water from his bottle and examined the junior children's paintings stuck up in a hallway. Bright gardens. Grinning sheep. Shiny happy people holding hands. And there were lots of paintings of the lake. One in particular stopped him. A four-year-old's take on Lough Linger; a splodge of blue and rising from the middle of it, a big human arm.

Ewan looked at the bottle in his hand.

Back in class there was an envelope on his bench. It smelled of vanilla. Before opening it Ewan glanced around. Only Andrew was near and he could not read these days. Ewan gave him the envelope to sniff at while he looked at the card. It was from Brigit but turned out to be a get well soon card for May. The message read, 'I hope you'll be back in class with us before long.'

Ewan doubted May would be back. A card from Brigit would hardly encourage her, surely Brigit realised that?

When school was done Ewan quick-stepped along until he caught up with her. This meant leaving Andrew behind but he could see that Mr Swift had his attention. They were standing together by the fruit trees, Mr Swift speaking quietly to the monster-boy.

'I'll give May the card,' Ewan said to Brigit, 'but I don't think you're her favourite person.'

'It's in your hands now,' said Brigit. 'I am sure you will do the right thing.'

Looking at her, Ewan got lost somewhere between the angle of her cheekbone and the soft upturn to her nose. There was a silent gap where Ewan did not know what to say. Amber Feather approached and filled it.

'Good afternoon,' she said to them both. 'Ewan, can we talk?'

'Ah . . . okay,' he said.

Brigit smiled and took leave of them. Ewan watched her glide away. Amber stepped into his view. 'Let's go get Andrew first,' she said.

'He'll be fine with Mr Swift a while,' said Ewan.

'I'm not so certain of that,' replied Amber. She was already walking up to the fruit trees. Mr Swift saw her approaching and stepped back from the monster-boy.

'Mr Swift,' Amber greeted him with a nod.

'Miss Feather,' he returned with a small bow.

Ewan strolled with the Mayor towards the lake-shore. Andrew stomped along behind them. He was not sure about this woman. She made sweet noises and he liked the way her hair sparkled but she had also taken him away from the old man with the stick. Andrew preferred the old man with the stick.

'Mr Swift is interested in Andrew,' said Amber.

'So are most people,' said Ewan.

'I'm not,' said Amber, 'I'm more interested in you. But I'd rather you didn't leave Andrew alone with him. Mr Swift gets eccentric ideas. That would be fine but he's also a bitter man.'

Ewan was shocked to hear this about the cheerful Mr Swift. He would have been surprised to hear it said about anyone in the valley. For that matter, it was surprising to hear any citizen of Lough Linger speak in such a way. He did not think they knew what

100

bitterness was. Perhaps it was the Mayor's duty to know about such things.

'It's all because he once loved a girl who didn't love him,' said Amber. 'Not enough, anyway. He never got over it. Most people in the village would say that Mr Swift is odd but harmless. I think it's more serious than that. I think he's angry and deeply resentful.'

'What could he possibly do to Andrew?' asked Ewan.

'It's more what he could do *with* him. Andrew is innocent and could be manipulated, but he's also powerful. Mr Swift first got interested in Andrew when he saw his strength, do you remember?'

'It was after Andrew smashed the pier that he invited us to stay,' said Ewan.

'That's right, I worry Mr Swift has taken against our community. He might want to use Andrew, put him up to vandalism or some other unpleasantness.'

Ewan glanced back at Andrew. 'Even if Mr Swift wanted to, Andrew is not that easy to control. He's stubborn. And I really don't think Mr Swift would use him anyway. He likes him too much. He came to fetch us when the Lesser-Spotted Blossom appeared—'

As soon as Ewan said that he remembered how it had ended. Andrew scared the plant back into the ground. *Could Mr Swift have been hoping that would happen?* Villagers were left disappointed. A bitter man might have enjoyed it.

Amber saw him remembering. 'Do you see what I mean?' she asked. 'But all we can do is keep an eye on him. I've no solid evidence that Mr Swift isn't to be trusted. The villagers would need to see evidence.'

'Then you could all persuade him to get some counselling,' said Ewan.

'Ah, Ewan,' said Amber, her face breaking into a smile, 'wanting the best for everyone. That's why I came to talk to you in the first place. I've been telling everyone that the Founder liked you. We all place great faith in the Founder's ability to judge character. It's starting to look like the village might be happy to have you longer. Everyone is charmed by you, the selfless way you take care of Andrew, the patience you have with May. The whole village has noticed. Your friends, I'm afraid, don't really fit here – but you're different. You're special.'

With her words Ewan felt a rush of warmth. A sense of being wanted. He had not experienced such a feeling in a long time. It was sad about Mr Swift. Lough Linger was not as ideal as it had first appeared but was still the best chance Ewan was going to get. 'Thanks!' he said.

12

Above, squirrels leaped from pine to pine. Below, beetles dug in fallen needles. May spent the day walking.

All was peaceful until the evening when she felt a ripple of panic pass through the trees. She stopped, listened and felt. There was a predator about. May looked up but could not see much open sky between the tightly planted pines. She communed with frightened blackbirds, trying to get a picture of the predator.

DangerousDangerDangerous

Then she saw it with her own eyes, a silvery shape flying over the treetops. May was not frightened of it. It was Theodora.

'Hey!' May jumped up and down, waving.

Theodora had already spotted her. She cruised back overhead, riding side-saddle on a shovel handle. She leaned on its tip, pressing it into descent. The handle's pointed end went into the ground and Theodora touched down. She pulled her goggles off her face and let them hang around her neck.

'Hello, May.'

There was something stern about Theodora's manner that made May giggle. 'How are ye getting on?' she asked.

'I'm doing fine,' said Theodora. Bits of straw were stuck in her mackintosh's buttonholes. Maybe she was sleeping in hay sheds.

May made a little shrug. 'Not much goin' on here,' she said. 'I'm still hanging around Lough Linger. Andrew's not cured yet . . .'

May's words trailed off. Theodora was beyond stern, she was staring at her, hard as steel. 'I saw what you did with those swans,' she said. 'How you used them against that bloke.'

So that was it. May bowed her head. She used the toes of her wellingtons to push little channels through the pine needles. 'Aye,' she said, 'he's me dad.'

'Your father?' said Theodora. 'You must really hate him.'

'Won't go that far,' said May, squirming under the interrogation and Theodora's relentless stare. Right then, in that lonely forest, it seemed to May that there was enough hate in the world. *DangerousDanger* was still coming to her from between the trees. The squirrels had cleared the area. The blackbirds were wheeling away. 'I just want him to leave me alone,' she explained.

'You didn't quite succeed,' said Theodora. She indicated backwards with her head. 'Your father is in the next valley. He's got a tent pitched. Looks like he's set-tling in for a while. I guess he's the determined type.'

'Might be,' said May. Actually, determination was the last thing she would have associated with her dad. Maybe he really had changed.

Theodora softened, just a fraction. 'I'd no idea your power was so . . . powerful,' she said.

'It's not so mighty really,' said May with a shrug. 'I can't switch it on and off. It's not a tool, it's more like a way of life.'

'I bet I could use it like a tool,' said Theodora.

'Ye reckon ye could do better than me?' said May. 'Me that's been at it for years?'

'I'd like to try,' said Theodora. 'I'd like you to give it to me.'

Was she serious? May giggled. 'No way,' she said.

'All you have to do is let me in,' Theodora said soothingly. 'I'll sweep it clean away. You'll be able to get on better without all that animal racket in your head.'

'No,' said May, 'I love it, it's the best thing I've got.'

'People love their faults as much as their good stuff,' Theodora sighed. 'We love to be *different*. But has being a freak ever made you happy? Do you think it ever will? Maybe it's time to try something new. Try quiet and normality.'

'I don't want to be ordinary,' May protested, 'I'm one of *us*, remember?'

'But you could have a nice life,' said Theodora. 'Nobody likes us weirdos, not really. It's too late for me but you can still join the human race. Let me take your ability and you'll be able to have normal friendships with people. Have a boyfriend someday maybe.'

'Ah!' said May, a noise that sounded both hurt and humorous. May constructed a smile on her face. She now knew that Theodora was serious. But she did not want her to know that she knew. She wanted to leave Theodora a way out of this. They did not have to fight. Theodora could still back off and they could be friends. They could go for a walk and talk and laugh and just be together.

'Go on, give it to me,' said Theodora. She extended one hand. 'I promise to do wonderful things with your power. You'll be able to watch.'

'No way,' said May with a fake giggle.

'*Please?*' said Theodora.

'I said no.'

'Go on, give it to me.'

This was too much. May felt herself folding under the weight of Theodora's personality. She glanced around although there was nothing to see. The light was fading. It was just the two of them in the plantation, in the midst of a thousand identical trees. May knew that Theodora could only take her ability if she let her. She just had to stay strong. Maybe it was time to get angry? Shout at her?

'No,' said May, 'please just forget it.' She was disappointed by the weakness in her own voice.

'Don't you want people to like you?' asked Theodora.

That was a mistake. May's chin went up. 'No,' she said, 'I don't care if people like me or not.'

Theodora paused, trying to reclaim advantage, trying to put doubt back into May. 'Not even Andrew,' she asked, her eyebrows up.

'He likes me for who I am,' said May.

'So you don't care that people think you're a freak,' said Theodora, as if speaking to an illogical child. 'The only person that doesn't is a freak himself.'

'That's right,' said May and she performed a confident laugh. It was not a great performance but May was still pretending that this conversation was just banter. Pretending she had not noticed that she was being cruelly bullied.

For a moment the only sound was the creak of trees.

'I want your power,' said Theodora. Her steel was back.

May shook her head stiffly, afraid if she spoke a wobble in her voice would betray her.

'I want it,' Theodora said coldly. She was in a more aggressive gear. Her fingers tightened around the shovel handle.

May received worry ... *DangerousDanger* ... *GetAwayFromHer* ... She could not identify any particular animal as source. It seemed the whole forest was thinking it. May looked right and left. It was almost dark now. The regularly spaced trees disappeared, row by row, into gloom.

'I want it,' said Theodora.

'No,' said May and her fear was obvious in her annunciation of even that tiny word.

'I want it.'

'No!' May shouted. She tried to hold down her dread. She felt around for animal help, there were beetles, badgers. Nothing big enough, nothing fast enough. What should she do? Scream? Get angry? Stomp away? Theodora was so used to getting what she wanted. *But not this time*, May toughened herself, *not this one little time*.

Now both Theodora's hands were around the shovel handle. She pulled it out of the soil and held it horizontal in front of her. Her feet left the ground. 'I'll give you twenty seconds to think about it,' she said. Then she dropped onto the handle and shot away between the pines. May was alone.

May decided she would not run back to the village. She would walk. She set off, it was a fast walk. Above the sound of her own breathing she heard a *whoosh*, first behind her then in front. She looked around but saw only tree trunks fading to black.

Whooooosh.

'Give it to me!' Theodora yelled as she rocketed past.

'No!' shouted May, spinning around. Theodora was gone already.

'I want it,' she heard Theodora calling from the distance, her voice sailing among the pines. 'I want it.'

May tried fury. 'NEVER,' she screamed. She walked faster. This was still not running, jogging maybe but definitely not running. Anything around that could help? She felt spiders, snails, a single blackbird—

Theodora was shooting straight at her. May caught a split second of her intense stare, in goggles, before hitting the ground. Theodora flew over. May felt the buckle of her mackintosh's hanging belt run the length of her back.

Quiet again.

Pine needles were pressed into May's face. She rubbed them off, looked around and her heart stopped. Theodora was hovering right behind her, perfectly at ease in the air. May's eyes locked on the handle's pointed tip. It was pointed her way, like a gun.

'Give it to me,' said Theodora.

She could only take the ability if May let her. May just had to be strong.

I will not cry, May told herself, *and I will not say please*.

'GIVE,' screamed Theodora. She helicoptered at May, spinning on the shovel handle. Its blunt end struck May's chest, her feet left the ground and she hit a tree.

Sinking down against the trunk, May tried to breathe. She was in shock. No one ever hit her before. Theodora soared to the treetops and looked down at the injured girl. Theodora was shaken by her actions too. Her elbows were jiggering so much she could not stay straight in her airspace. Theodora had terrified herself with her own ferocity but that did not make May feel better. It just meant that Theodora was completely out of control. She was beyond even her own control, all inhibition was gone. If Theodora was to admit any trace of humanity now she would also have to admit that she had become a brute. She was liable to do anything instead of that. Not even Theodora knew what.

May got up.

This was definitely running.

Branches tore at her dress and face. She cut diagonally across the tree lanes. Theodora had to swing, like a pendulum, in and out to stay on May's trail. *HelpHelpHelpHelp*. Worms, squirrels— *Ah!* Red deer. A whole bachelor party of stags were on the slopes above the plantation. Already their noses were raised, attentive to May's distress. They broke into gallops.

May glanced and there was Theodora, riding sidesaddle two rows away and keeping up with May easily. She loosened one hand and waved. Theodora had obviously gone completely psycho. She mouthed the words, 'Give it to me,' then cut in front.

May dug her heels in, pine needles sprayed right

and left and she landed on her back. Silvery hair and mackintosh twirled in the air above. The handle's point plunged into the ground by May's ear and Theodora was standing over her. Behind her goggles, Theodora's eyes were dilated to an inhuman extent. 'That was fun,' she said, breathing heavily.

Where were the deer? Red deer would soon wipe the smile off her face.

May listened for the pounding of hooves but instead felt frustration. The deer were bucking at the edge of the plantation but could not enter. It was their antlers, they were too wide to pass between the closely planted pines. They felt May's fright but could not help. She was on her own.

Do not cry, May told herself, *and do not say please*.

She rolled from under Theodora and ran again. Theodora allowed her a five-second start before mounting the handle and zooming after her. May could hear her shrieking as she swept closer. She dodged into a parallel route, Theodora shot past and disappeared into darkness.

Seven seconds later she came back screaming, 'GIVE!'

Theodora side-slammed her. May bounced between trees like a pinball. Blood and sap mixed in her mouth. Her brain hissed with static. But a moment later May was running swiftly away. So swiftly that May could hardly believe it herself. She tried to focus on her feet, they were working by themselves. May must have been running on automatic, her instincts in charge. It was amazing.

May realised the ground was getting further away.

Then she realised that Theodora's arm was wrapped around her waist.

May's feet were not running, they were kicking. Theodora was lifting her into the air.

'Let go of me!' May shouted. She struggled to break Theodora's grip as the view around them changed.

Those were treetops.

That was the whole plantation.

This was high.

May threw her arms around Theodora and clung to her. Higher, higher they went, above the village. May smelled chimney smoke. The villagers were down there, cosy in their homes and innocent of the fight above. Higher, higher, the lake surface was black and smooth. Soon Theodora had brought her higher than the hills. The air was flawless and pristine, never furrowed before. The only sound was the flapping of Theodora's mackintosh. May sobbed into her arm.

'Please put me down,' she cried.

'Give it to me and I will,' Theodora whispered into her ear. May hugged her with a loving intensity that was actually the fear of falling. She imagined being skewered on a pine tree or hitting granite so fast her body would instantly liquefy, leaving nothing but a damp patch and a pair of wellingtons.

'Please,' May managed to say.

They were hung in the middle of the night sky. May could see the world revolving beneath them. The whole mountain range and the lowlands beyond, laid out like a map drawn on black paper. The clots of light represented towns and villages. Moving light dots were cars creeping along. Her dad was somewhere down there too. So many people hugging the earth and none of them knew a thing.

'Give it to me,' whispered Theodora.

Hung in the silence they looked into each other's eyes. They breathed each other's breath.

May jerked her head back and said, 'Not ever.'

So Theodora dropped her.

Through her ability May had felt the sensation of flight more keenly than most humans ever do. She had lived it via birds. She knew the feeling of solid air under wings. She had experienced the sky as a place that could be travelled rather than a vast untouchable. She knew what it was like to fly. But this right now, this was not flying. This was falling. The only place May was travelling was a narrow tube leading straight to the earth's surface. She travelled it fast.

Flat darkness below.

Darkness all around.

Feet first, May pierced the skin of Lough Linger. Water shot up her nose and slammed her brain. She was driven down, slowing by the metre, until her feet

113

hit the bottom. There she stood, her hair and clothes waving. The water was so clear that the faint starlight was enough to draw a gleam from the granite lakebed. Lough Linger was like a moon's crater, only full of water. She was almost in the centre of its great stone bowl. It was spotless, not a single piece of weed or crawling life. Above, she could see things hovering in mid-water, but there was no time to think about them.

May had never learned to swim.

Her drowning had already begun.

Up.

May kicked up. The water activated around, her life escaping in bubbles and streaming up. She tried to catch up.

Up.

This was sink or swim. This was die or live. This was down or . . .

UpUp

Up on Lough Linger's surface a few air bubbles popped and were gone. Nothing else happened for a while. The reflection of stars slinked this way and that on the dark surface. Lough Linger was always calm but it did, almost imperceptibly, heave to an extremely slow rhythm, like a giant thing asleep. But now Lough Linger crashed open. Gasping, May clutched at the sky. She saw the village lights far away. Too far. She was in the middle of the lake. Then she went under and lake clamped shut over her head again.

UpUpUp

Again May broke the surface, up almost to her waist. She flapped her arms but sank again.

UP

Water crashed over her shoulders as she re-emerged. This time she stayed up. May stood there, out to her ankles. Water sloshed over her wellingtons' brims. Her hair and clothes clung to her. She beheld the dark lake and the hills all around. She took a breath and told herself to be still. May did not raise her arms in a gesture of thanks. Instead a deep gratitude rose inside her, nudging the bottom of her heart.

May's first steps were slow. Each footfall sank under the surface but found support and bopped back up. May got more confident and headed for shore. She walked on water.

Lough Linger's fish lay before her, as big and sub-servient as logs. Their scales glinted under the surface. They had pushed her up and would now carry her to land. They sank behind the girl and rose before her, pumping their bodies to keep her supported and pleased to be her stepping stones.

May stepped ashore. She was on the opposite bank from the village. There was no sigh of anybody, just the dark woods. May sat on a rock and hugged her knees. There she waited out the night.

13

Theodora Farr had come a long way. It had always been remarked that she was an especially sensitive child. Even during her baptism her serenity was noted. As a toddler she never cried or fought. Her first word was 'lake'. Other five-year-olds chased butterflies. Theodora just extended her hand and the butterflies came to her, attracted by her sweetness. On her eighth birthday Amber Feather, recently elected Mayor, brought her a gift. Identifying potential Brides was part of the Mayor's job and everyone noticed this mark of special regard. From then on Theodora was treated differently. Inside herself, the young Theodora felt something else that was different too. Later she would realise it was a supernatural ability and she would learn to use it. In the meantime she believed it was just another symptom of her blessedness. When not studying or doing good deeds Theodora was on the lakeshore with a dreamy look on her face. Her twelfth birthday was attended by every citizen of

Lough Linger. They all said she glowed with purity. That evening Theodora went to her parents and told them, 'I want to be a Bride of the Lake.'

Theodora was dressed in linen robes and had flowers plaited in her hair. She was brought to the Founder. Never had the villagers been so certain of a soul receiving approval. Theodora would be declared a Bride of the Lake and moved into the tower, as had always been her destiny. Her meeting with the Founder was just a formality. Amber Feather ushered Theodora into his chamber. The Founder's eyes slid open and studied the latest offering. He took her hand. The only sound was the loud suction of his breath. His fingers had the power to probe deeper than mere skin, everybody knew that. They accessed your very soul.

The Founder dropped her hand and said, 'Sorry, no.'

Amber stared, as if this might be a joke. 'Theodora's as good a girl as ever grew up by Lough Linger,' she said.

'Not in my opinion,' said the Founder, 'and my opinion is what counts. I know what is acceptable to Uncle. And this girl is not.'

Theodora felt her whole world tip under her feet. This was not how it was supposed to be. She had kept her soul spotless. She was not the person the Founder thought she was. And if she was that person . . . then who was she?

'Please,' she cried. 'I'll do anything!' She felt so stupid standing there in those robes. All dressed up and nowhere to go.

'No approval,' said the Founder. 'Not ever.'

The gentle folk of the valley were as decent as ever. There was nothing to stop Theodora staying in Lough Linger until she died of old age. But her heart was broken. One night, as the village slept, she took the *Bridal Sweet* and rowed out into the middle of the lake. There she waited and waited. But Uncle did not rise. Its hand did not reach for her. Ashamed, she rowed back to the village at dawn. A few months later she ran away.

Theodora had never been out of the valley before. It was an education. She spent three years on the road and on the street. She discovered her ability and the abilities of other girls. She learned to use them. Every night, no matter where she was, alley, hostel or open field, she thought of Lough Linger. It did not please her to think of it. Her homesickness was mainly just sickness. She felt a nauseous spite from head to toe, it kept her warm at night. Theodora was born to be a Bride of the Lake. Then the Founder had told her 'no', but nobody told her what to be instead. Nobody offered her an alternative meaning to her existence. Very well, she would come up with one herself.

Now Theodora was back. She had been watching Lough Linger for over a week. Dawn was inching into the valley. Her mackintosh flapped, her silvery hair streamed in the breeze. May had been tougher than she expected so now Theodora was looking for something else. Something else she could use.

Andrew shook Ewan awake. Squealing, Ewan fought to get away and fell out of bed. Andrew had almost dislocated his shoulder.

'What!?' Ewan demanded from the floor. A bruise in the shape of Andrew's thumb bloomed on his arm.

Andrew pointed to May's empty bed. She was gone all night.

Ewan rubbed his injury. 'So what?' he complained. 'She's probably asleep in a badger's burrow or something. She's always doing things like that.'

Ewan got back in bed and pulled his quilt over his head. It was only dawn yet. But Andrew would not let Ewan alone. He kept shuffling around the guest house and banging into things. Eventually Ewan sat up. 'I suppose you want to go out,' he said.

Ewan had noticed that the people of Lough Linger were late risers. The whole village seemed to sleep until ten. They walked between silent cottages towards the jetty. Ewan stopped in his tracks. They were not first up after all. The brothers Early were already there, casting their fishing lines.

Okay, nobody likes fishing that much, Ewan thought.
He turned Andrew around and brought him along

the path to their other regular drinking spot, outside the village between the two massive boulders. Andrew hunched by the water. Ewan climbed a boulder and looked back at the men on the jetty. The brothers' constant presence there was finally making him uneasy. May was right. Completely wacko was what it was.

When he looked back around, Andrew was cowering against the rock, shielding his face with his hands. A girl in a cream-coloured mackintosh was standing over him. How had she gotten there without Ewan seeing? And why was Andrew so frightened of her? She had a section of wooden banister in her hands but that was no threat to Andrew. He could have used it as a toothpick. The girl was examining him closely, scanning his back and big arm.

'Careful,' Ewan advised, 'he doesn't like being touched by strangers.'

The girl glanced up at him. 'He keeps trying to drink,' she said, 'but the lake water won't let him swallow it. Did you notice that?'

Ewan had not noticed, so he held his hands together in front of him and said nothing.

'His infection,' Theodora continued, studying Andrew but speaking to Ewan, 'it's not *normal* is it?'

'So little is these days,' replied Ewan.

The girl had a great answer to that. She held the banister behind her and sat on it. Next thing she was

120

hovering. The girl ascended to Ewan's level. Elevation came easy to her, she showed no sign of mental concentration. Andrew shrank away and whimpered at the sight of a human in flight. His mind had difficulty with normal things, the impossible caused him terrible anxiety. The girl floated over and stepped onto the boulder. Then she swung the banister up under her elbows. Completely relaxed, she leaned back as if the banister was still in a house rather than floating mid-air. All this was astounding but Ewan played it cool. May had hinted that her new friend was special, like her, but not in which way. Now he knew.

'You're Theodora,' said Ewan.

'Correct,' said Theodora. 'You're Ewan.'

'I am,' said Ewan. 'And you grew up here.'

'Correct,' said Theodora. 'You came seeking a cure for your big friend.'

'We did,' said Ewan. 'But you hate this place now.'

'Correct,' said Theodora. 'And you're realising that Andrew will never be fixed by this lake.'

'I am,' said Ewan. 'And there's a giant living in the lake.'

'Correct,' said Theodora. She paused a fraction of a second. 'How'd you know that?'

'I was kind of guessing,' said Ewan, 'until now.'

Theodora threw her head back and laughed, the banister dipping down before bouncing up again. She liked this boy. He was someone she could deal with. Not bad-looking, either. Gentle eyes, sad somehow, looking out like the last puppy in a pet shop. She smiled at him, waiting to see what he would say next.

'What does it look like?' asked Ewan.

'Sorta human-looking,' said Theodora. 'A kind of angel. When I was a kid I imagined a big person lying at the bottom of the lake with wings folded over their back. Just lying there, being gorgeous and holding their breath for months. I was totally in love. We've all seen the giant arm reaching out from the middle of the lake. It's human, but Uncle would need to be ten metres tall to have an arm like that.'

'Uncle?' said Ewan.

'That's what they call it,' said Theodora, 'although no one knows if it's a boy or a girl. Hundreds of years ago everyone just assumed it was a bloke. Later, people complained, saying it could just as likely be female. So everyone took to referring to the giant as *it*, although the title Uncle stuck. Also, it used to be that only girls went to Uncle. That's why they're called Brides. It was dead sexist in those days. But it's been equal opportunities for ages now, boys can be Brides too.'

'The Brides go to Uncle?'

'Yes,' said Theodora. 'Uncle keeps the water in Lough Linger blessed, but there's a price. It gets the Brides of the Lake in return. Uncle likes them young.

Old enough to be responsible but young enough to have always done the right thing and kept their souls squeaky clean. Around fifteen, no older.'

'My friends and I are that age,' said Ewan.

Theodora winked at him. 'That's a ripe age around here,' she said.

'How do you know if someone's soul is good enough?' asked Ewan.

This was a sensitive subject. Theodora surprised herself by the stinging in her tear ducts when reminded of the Founder and the way he had rejected her. It was the Founder who could tell if a soul would be good enough for Uncle. He had rejected hers and had been proved right. All night she had sat out on the lake and Uncle did not go near her. Theodora had put a lot of work into suppressing the memory of her rejection. She did not want to talk about it. So Theodora did not tell Ewan how the Brides of the Lake were identified. She did not tell him that you were brought to meet the Founder. She did not tell him how he probed your soul when your hand was in his. Theodora did not mention the Founder at all. That was too bad. Ewan would have been interested.

Ewan saw Theodora was unwilling so he quickly moved on. He did not want to lose her, she was a great source of information. 'What does Uncle do with the Brides?' he asked.

'It takes them under the lake,' said Theodora, recovering. 'That's all we know. None have ever come back.'

Ewan looked across the water. Flat, silent, deep.

'Most believe the Brides go and live under the lake with Uncle,' said Theodora. 'That's what we were taught as kids. Our village needed Uncle to keep the lake good and we knew Uncle needed the Brides. But it was not a frightening idea. Plenty of us were queuing up to try and become Brides. It made us sad that Uncle was lonely but we also wanted the honour of being chosen. We wanted to be the one with the finest soul. We imagined there was another world down there, a big air bubble where the best souls lived happily ever after. Wherever Uncle put the Brides, it was bound to be wonderful.'

'They go to Uncle on that boat?' Ewan asked. He pointed to the *Bridal Sweet*, still upside down on the jetty.

'That's right,' said Theodora. 'A couple of times a year it's decided that Uncle wants a new friend. That's how it starts – it's the only way I've ever seen it start. They say, in the past, Uncle has been hurt and needed a Bride to be soothed but nobody's seen that, it hasn't happened in centuries. The oldest Bride, they'll be living in the tower by then, is paraded to the jetty at sunset. It's a big ritual. The whole village takes part. The Bride stands on the boat and is pushed out. We watch Uncle's hand reach up, take hold of the Bride and pull them under. Everyone applauds. Celebrations can go on all night.'

'The whole village takes part?'

'Everybody,' Theodora confirmed. 'Every citizen of Lough Linger.'

Villagers' faces flicked over in Ewan's head like a slide show. Mrs Honeyford, Farmer Able, Miss Boswell, the Hopkins, all smiling. Carrick, Amber, Betty, the Humes, all gentle and generous. All his classmates. The teachers. The farm workers. The shopkeepers. Everybody, the whole village. Ewan spread his feet, afraid his dizziness would cause him to fall off the boulder. He pictured the villagers in the dark, standing close together by the shore, entranced by the sight of a Bride sent drifting out. Or perhaps not entranced at all, perhaps merry, drinking tea and speaking fondly of Uncle. Another pleasant evening in Lough Linger, gathered together to kill one of their own children.

'I can promise you this,' said Ewan, 'Uncle is not an angel. The Brides aren't living forever at the bottom of the lake. They're dead. They've been sacrificed.' He stared back at the village. 'I should have known. They have *so much*. They live *so long*. Someone had to be paying. Someone is always paying.'

Theodora challenged him, 'An expert, are you?'

'Yes,' said Ewan. 'I've been sacrificed myself.'

125

'You seem well enough,' said Theodora.

'I managed to escape. Otherwise I'd not be well at all.'

Theodora shrugged. 'You've obviously seen some bad stuff,' she said. 'It's easy for you to not believe that Uncle is kind and caring. But these people . . .' She waved towards the village. 'Their lives are endless sweetness and light. They'll never believe Uncle is a murderer.'

'Not really a murderer,' said Ewan. 'A monster. A thing that lives on the suffering of others. Who's the next Bride?'

'Her name's Brigit,' said Theodora. 'Nice girl, head in the clouds though.'

'Brigit!' Ewan said and for a moment he tasted vanilla. 'I'll save her!'

'Look at you, Mister Hero!' Theodora laughed. 'I'm sure you'll sweep her off her feet.'

Ewan jumped down from the boulder. 'Come on, Andrew,' he said, 'we're going.'

Andrew peeped out from between his fingers. He was still cowering from the flying girl.

She turned on her heels and leaned out over the boys, supported by the floating banister. They had to pass beneath her to leave but Andrew refused. Frightened of the girl, he would not even stand up straight. Ewan tried to shove him onwards. He might as well have tried to shift one of the boulders.

Theodora got a chuckle from the trouble she was causing. 'You might fancy doing something for Brigit,' she said. 'But May would do anything, *anything*, for Andrew.'

Ewan gave up shoving. All the air went out of him with a wheeze. He looked at the back of Andrew's neck. Big, solid Andrew. May trusted him completely, even with his monster infection. That only increased her devotion. 'Yes, it's true,' he said.

There was a gust and when he looked Theodora was gone.

14

The villagers arose from their beds. They each drank a glass of water. It did not taste of centuries of sacrifice. It tasted of love. Everyone stood for a moment, feeling the sun on their faces, before sweeping their front doorsteps. The tea shop opened. Kids played games. Workers went whistling to their fields or plantations. The older folks switched on their radios. Miss Boswell started baking, the smell of almonds hung around her. Mr Merriman wrote a list, nothing if not organised. Wilma Wright clipped her herbs, chubby, pink and content. Everyone loved Uncle. They were filled with well-being when they thought of its sublime presence in the lake. Uncle: gentle, kind and ten metres tall.

The boys found May standing in the guest house. Andrew made a happy gurgle as soon as he saw her. He did not register her scratches and bruising. It appeared May really had slept in a badger's burrow. Her hair was tangled and dirty. Her dress was torn in several places. Ewan saw May's state but did not let it distract him. 'I've found out what's going on,' he said. 'There's some kind of monster in the lake. The villagers are sacrificing kids to it. Fifteen-year-olds with pure souls.'

'There's no monster in that lake,' May said assuredly.

'Your friend Theodora told me,' said Ewan.

'She's not me friend!'

'Whatever she is, she grew up here and she knows,' said Ewan, 'I believe her.'

'I was in the lake last night, all the way to the bottom,' said May. 'If there was a monster I'd have felt it. I felt nothing but fish.'

That stopped Ewan. He sought explanations. 'Perhaps you couldn't feel it because it's part human,' he suggested. 'Or perhaps it was hiding?'

'That would be a great monster, wouldn't it?' said May. 'Scared of me! I'm even the right age. Why didn't this creature go for me, then?'

Ewan said nothing, but his face must have spoken.

'Me soul wasn't good enough?' said May. 'That's what you're thinking, isn't it?'

'No, of course not,' said Ewan, but without much conviction.

'I don't care what ye think,' said May.

Andrew detected May's sore heart. He whimpered in sympathy. May twisted her fingers together, pulled them apart and twisted them together again. 'I don't believe in souls anyway,' she said.

Ewan shook his head furiously. He wanted their attention on the immediate problem. 'I don't know why you didn't feel it and I don't know why it didn't come after you,' he said. 'But I know this – Brigit is in danger and we must help her.'

'Brigit is the most conceited person I've ever meet in me life,' said May. 'It's only Andrew who needs our help.'

'Can't you just forget Andrew for two minutes?'

'No! He's the reason we're here.'

'He's why *you're* here perhaps,' said Ewan. 'I came here because I had to go somewhere. I am trying . . . Just trying to *be something*.'

'Aye,' said May. 'And do ye know what your problem is? What your problem has always been? Ye can't stand it that you're not special.'

Ewan recoiled as if smacked. 'It's easy for you with your ability,' he said. 'Even Andrew is special in his way. And he's got a home. But I have nothing, nobody and nowhere to go.'

He turned and stalked out.

The neat gardens, the gleaming whitewash, even the sun itself made him sick. Ewan walked unsteadily. He thought a wasp was buzzing at his ear and he batted it away. But there was no wasp. It was the sound of Mrs Melody's fiddle playing. He thought he could smell rot underlying the baking bread and roses. That community centre, those cute cottages, they were all built on foundations of abuse. The lake itself seemed to glint with evil. A flock of children ran past him on the track, flying a kite. Older villagers were leaning against their gateposts, all content and full of chat. They often turned their heads and gazed at the lake, remarking on how wonderful it looked. The villagers, Ewan now realised, were always looking at the lake. Every spare moment it was where their eyes rested. Ewan walked stiffly between them, trying to find the route most likely to avoid encounters. He kept his head down, trying to be small, feeling queasy and mad.

'Toodle-pip.' Mrs Hume was standing in front him. Her thick lenses made her eyes the size of saucers. Automatically, Ewan leaned away from her.

'Where are you hurrying to this fine morning?' she asked.

'Nowhere,' said Ewan. He regretted his defensive tone. *Act normal.*

'Would you like a pancake?'

'No . . . thank you, Mrs Hume.'

'They're tasty!' she insisted, inclining forwards on her toes. Her expression was supposed to be friendly but Ewan saw only a frightful leer. He could not speak, he was afraid of slapping her well-fed face or just vomiting right there on her shoes. He dashed away. Mrs Hume watched him go, curiously.

Ewan got away from the village and marched towards the Bride's tower, leaving the path and plunging into the plantation. He was glad to have escaped the villagers but, if he looked over his shoulder, he could still see the lake glinting between the trees. His fight with May replayed in his mind, more stinging every time. She was only interested in what suited her aims. Her mind was closed to everything else.

No wonder she prefers Andrew, he thought, *he never talks back*.

Ewan knew the tower was close but he was hemmed in by tall trees and it was difficult to spot. He blundered about a while, getting more and more frustrated. When he eventually did find the tower he cursed in anger. It was surrounded by a high circular wall. Why? Burglary in Lough Linger? Not likely. Then he noticed that the wall had another use. It was decorated from top to bottom. Glass pebbles and ceramic tiles were pressed into the crumbling plaster. The mosaic was old, probably older than the community centre's stained glass window. Many pieces had fallen out but Ewan could see the beginning of some words and above them the image of feet, resting sideways. He followed the wall and found legs, a torso and a pair of wings. He marched all the way around. Almost back at the feet, was Uncle's face, the size of a window. Its head was resting in its arms. Uncle was smiling benignly and gazing out from under mellow, half-closed eyelids, as if waking from a nap. Ewan sneered at it. The phrase written around the base of the wall was, 'We love Uncle and Uncle loves us'.

The Brides were given to Uncle all right. Even in life, the wall embraced their home so that the creature was wrapped around them day and night. At the same time, to outsiders, the mosaic said *what's in here is mine*. The village probably thought the mosaic was a lovely thing. To Ewan it was offensive.

They were not worried about burglary after all. Set in the wall by Uncle's elbow was a heavy wooden door. Not only was the door unlocked, it was not even fitted with a lock. Ewan took another look at Uncle's face and felt his blood run hot. Out loud he said, 'Lies.'

He kicked the door open and caused panic among some goats inside. They scattered and Ewan marched across the lawn. There was a swing set and a BMX bicycle lying on its side. There was a pet peacock and a few rows of pear trees. The tower was in the middle of the compound. It was wrapped in grape vines and ivy. Ewan pushed in the door and strode so fast up the spiral staircase he made himself dizzy. Brigit's room was highest. He burst in. A window overlooked the lake. There was a stereo and an armchair. Fluffy pillows and about forty soft toys covered the bed. Dried flowers hung from the beams. Brigit was at her desk looking up, not alarmed, more curious. She waited for Ewan to explain himself.

Ewan was panting from his dash up the tower. 'Pack a bag,' he said. 'I am getting you out of here.'

Brigit just stared.

'You're next to be given to Uncle,' said Ewan. 'Did you know that?'

Brigit stared another while, then said, 'Of course I did. That's why I've got the best room.'

Ewan grimaced at the soft furnishings.

'And I am not being *given*,' Brigit added. 'I go willingly.'

'You're being sacrificed to a creature's hunger,' said Ewan walking towards her across the room. 'You have to believe me. Monsters are real. I've seen them.'

'I am sorry to hear that.' Brigit sat still as a statue, never blinking. Only her lips moved. 'But I trust Uncle is not one of them.'

'Listen to me,' said Ewan, 'you're being fooled. You're not going to get hugged by some jolly blue giant. You are being fed to it. It won't be *nice*. I should have known this place was too good to be true. All your neighbours want Uncle to keep the lake water strong and rising. But Uncle has to get its energy from somewhere. Someone has to pay. Your neighbours are murdering you to make their lives longer and easier.'

'There is no crime in Lough Linger,' said Brigit, 'our Uncle makes sure of that.'

'Brigit! Everything you have and everything you could ever have will be taken from you. You will DIE.'

Brigit moved for the first time, looking out to the waters of Lough Linger. 'I know,' she said softly.

Ewan opened his mouth and closed it again. That had thrown him. Brigit already knew she would not live with Uncle forever. 'You know?' he said.

'Yes,' said Brigit. 'I've had plenty of time to consider it. Please do not think I am stupid.' She glanced at Ewan. 'I know what Uncle wants. It wants my life.'

'Let it *want*,' said Ewan. 'You've got rights, human rights, no one can force you to sacrifice yourself.'

'We owe Uncle everything,' said Brigit. 'No one is making me to do this. I volunteered. It is the highest honour in the valley.'

'An honour to die so everyone else can have an easy life?' said Ewan. His voice became cracked. It was agonising to be faced with such impervious faith. Why could Brigit not understand what was so plain to him?

Why could Ewan not understand what was so plain to her?

Brigit shook her head. 'An honour to be held in Uncle's hand,' she explained. 'An honour to feel, even for a moment, such perfect goodness.'

'There's nothing *good* about it,' said Ewan. 'Uncle is a monster. It eats kids and sweats fertiliser. You're being used.' He lurched forwards, going to seize Brigit's hand. But she whipped her hand away, the fastest move he had ever seen her make. He retreated a step, his heart seeming to slow, his blood becoming sluggish. Brigit looked at Ewan, sorrowful that he could not see the profound cycle she saw aglow everywhere she looked. Maybe it was too late for him. Maybe he had spent too much time with concrete and cruelty. It was sad that this boy could not tune into life's mysteries. Their mere mention offended his logic. 'I should not expect an outsider to understand,' she said.

'No, the problem is that you're too much of an insider,' said Ewan. 'The world is much bigger than this valley.'

'Our world is this valley,' said Brigit, 'and Uncle is its heart. Soon I will go to it. Sometimes in the evening I stand on my bed and imagine I am on the *Bridal Sweet*, floating out on the lake. I imagine Uncle's arm reaching up. I imagine its hand wrapped around me. I imagine it so hard that I lose my breath. I fall to my knees and I cry. I cry with joy.'

There was a long empty moment. Ewan's shoulders sagged.

Outside, the sun shone. Birds sang. The lake glinted.

Ewan could say no more. There was no more to say. His frustration was gone. Instead there was sadness. He turned on one foot and left. Slowly and heavily he threaded back down the steps. Outside the tower Amber Feather was sitting in the swing and waiting for him.

'I hope we aren't going to fight about this,' she said.

136

15

A cheerful rap on the guest house door was accompanied by a cheerful call. 'Hello, just visiting!' The latch hopped open and Mr Swift entered. He smiled all about him. 'There you are,' he said to Andrew, who was sitting on the floor. Then a flash of surprise crossed Mr Swift's face. The television had been kicked in, parts ripped out and twisted into knots. Andrew was sitting among the wreckage.

'Sorry about that,' said May from the couch. 'There was no stopping him.'

Andrew looked at the nice man with the stick and made an embarrassed sound.

'No problem, no problem at all,' said Mr Swift, regaining his jolliness. He poked at ripped wires with the tip of his cane. 'In fact, the urge to self-educate is to be encouraged. You wanted to see how it worked, didn't you, Andrew?'

May smiled. 'That's right,' she said.

'We've missed you in school, May,' Mr Swift said to her.

'Really?' she said.

Mr Swift had hardly glanced at her since arrival. He could not take his eyes off Andrew. He walked around the monster-boy, admiring his bulging neck.

'Would you like to come for a walk, Andrew?' he asked.

'Not a bad idea,' said May. 'It's good to tire him out.' She began to pull on her wellingtons.

'I'd be glad to take him myself,' Mr Swift hurried to say. 'Maybe you'd like a break?'

May stopped, one boot still off. She stretched both arms over the top of the couch. 'Andrew doesn't like it when I'm not around,' she said, 'he gets stressed.'

'Of course,' said Mr Swift.

They walked out together. There was a pleased perk to Andrew's lumber. *Old Man With Stick = Good. May = Good.* These were two people he liked being around. They did not care if he belched or banged into things. Andrew would gladly lumber around with them all day.

May did not want to go into a plantation and Mr Swift wanted to stay out of the village so they took a middle path across the fields. Mr Swift was not so chirpy anymore. It was clear he did not want May along. They stopped at a vantage point. Andrew did not care for looking at views, he stomped into a field and ate a cabbage. May and Mr Swift watched a gathering of villagers by the lake. They sang together and, in-between, talked, laughed and drank lake water from ladles. What looked from a distance like a cloth parcel was being handed around and fussed over.

'Someone's had a baby,' explained Mr Swift.

Andrew pulled up another cabbage and bit a lump out of it. The cabbages gave his jaws satisfying work but they made him strangely gloomy too. A tad lonely. He did not know it but the cabbages were reminding him of home.

Watching Mr Swift closely May said, 'Are they goin' to sacrifice the baby?'

If the teacher was shocked or alarmed by May's question he gave no sign of it. 'No,' he said, flatly, as if her question was just dumb. 'They're going to baptise it.'

Maybe Mr Swift was just a good actor. May looked at his polished shoes, quaint suit and unnecessary cane. He certainly looked like an actor. He was watching the baptism but May thought that was just to avoid her eye. Maybe there was something to Ewan's theory about a monster in the lake. Ewan was smart. But she was not about to tell Mr Swift anything. If Ewan was right then no villager was to be trusted.

'Ye lot get baptised in the lake?' she asked.

'Of course,' said Mr Swift with a sigh, 'we are taught to love the lake from birth.'

'Chapels are where it's usually done.'

'Lough Linger is our chapel. We get married by the lake too.'

'Are ye married?'

There was a long pause before Mr Swift said, 'I have not had that good fortune.'

'Didn't find the right girl, eh?'

Another pause. 'I found her all right . . . but—' He swallowed.

Mr Swift's discomfort only encouraged May. 'Went off with another fella, did she?'

'In a manner of speaking,' he said.

'Huh? Manners?'

Mr Swift sniffed. 'It was a long time ago,' he said. 'We were only about your age. We both wanted different things. She left. She went to be with her Uncle.'

'Ye must have been mad.'

'Yes,' said Mr Swift. 'In fact, I've come to hate that Uncle with my entire soul.' As he said those words Mr Swift stabbed the tip of his cane into the ground. Rage radiated from him. May was startled and impressed. She had never seen any citizen of Lough Linger behave like this. She did not think they had it in them. She no longer wanted to annoy Mr Swift. It seemed you only had to scratch his cheery surface to find something seething inside.

'Is the girl still living?' she asked.

'Some like to say so. But I doubt it.'

A song reached them on the air. Everyone by the lake was singing again.

'Wouldn't ye like to be at this do as well?' asked May, indicating the ritual. 'They'll be wondering where ye are.'

'They won't miss me,' said Mr Swift. 'It's the Mayor's absence they'll be wondering about.' He pointed with his cane. Amber Feather and Ewan were walking through the village. They had bypassed the baptism and there was something severe in their strides. May recognised Ewan's *I-mean-business* walk, hands behind his back, brow intense, fifteen going on fifty. All four of them saw one another. Everybody looked but nobody waved. Between them all ran threads of distrust.

When they had gone Mr Swift said, 'I don't tend to join citizen gatherings like baptisms. Everyone is used to my peculiar ways. To be honest, most of them think I'm soft-in-the-head.'

May squinted up at Mr Swift. She opened her mouth and just came out with it. 'Ewan reckons there's a monster in the lake,' she said.

Mr Swift met her eye now. May's small face was pinched up, this was serious. She had a thoughtless defiance that he suddenly liked. Mr Swift knew he spent too much time lost in thought. His ideas and plans were more real to him than his actual surroundings. The memory of his lost love was more real than his closest neighbours. Looking at May now he felt the sudden jolt of her existence. Before she had just been a set of impressions, cheeky remarks and a strong accent. Now she came into focus and he realised that she was actually remarkable. She was more alive than he had been in a century.

'Monster?' he said thoughtfully. He longed to tell her the truth.

But no, no. It could not be.

'I haven't heard of any monster,' he said to May.

Mr Swift would not endanger his plot by telling this girl anything he did not need her to know. That included the existence of the thing in the lake. Mr Swift saw that May was devoted to Andrew. She would never allow him to be put at risk. But Mr Swift intended putting the monster-boy at risk. He planned to put Andrew in deep and deadly danger.

16

Mrs Honeyford checked the timer. The visitor's pies would soon be ready. She fixed it for all the pies to come out together even though Andrew's was far bigger. Mrs Honeyford had four sons of school-going age and was used to large portions. She drank a pint of water while looking out at the source. The lake was smooth as glass, not a single ripple to untidy the effect. Mrs Honeyford knew that in other places people actually got into lakes. They lowered themselves in and pushed with their arms and legs. Moving through water like fish. Imagine!

No one swam in Lough Linger. Uncle was entitled to its personal space.

What Mrs Honeyford liked was walking. She had formed the Lough Linger Walking Society. Once a week, she and other ladies donned their colourful lightweight jackets and sensible boots. They set off with high-tech anti-shock poles in one hand and plastic water bottles in the other. They kept off the hilltops, staying well within the valley as rainclouds might occasionally slip in and dampen spirits. They walked around the lake, picnicking at the far shore and coming back again. Almost always, they went around in a clockwise direction. But sometimes, gripped by spontaneity, they would head off around the lake in an anticlockwise direction. Those were days to remember.

Thump.

Mrs Honeyford jumped with fright. Her glass of water smashed on the tiles. Something had struck her roof.

May tried not to care that Ewan was missing all day. Last time she saw him he was walking with the Mayor. He had not returned to the guest house since. May went to the window and looked out. She could go ask some villagers if they had seen him but she hated the idea of needing their help.

A bass vibration passed through the guest house, filling every room. It sounded like an earthquake. It was Andrew's stomach rumbling.

Normally Ewan went to fetch their meals. May did not know where to go to get them. She did not even know who prepared the food. She looked out of the window again. Where was he?

Ruuuuummmmble.

Eventually there was nothing for it. May went out

and got directed to the Honeyfords' cottage. She was almost at the door when a shadow passed over. She froze. With a *thump* Theodora dropped onto the thatch. She leaned against the chimney. Today her power of flight was focused through a walking stick.

'Go away,' said May.

'I won't be staying long,' said Theodora, glancing to check no villagers had spotted her. 'How's your big friend?'

'None of your business.'

A village cat leaped up onto the thatch and hissed at Theodora. She kept it at bay with the walking stick. 'Relax the zoo-keeping a minute,' she said to May.

Other cats shot through their cat flaps and headed in their direction. May's power was rounding up every cat in the village.

'I'll tell you how Andrew is,' said Theodora, keeping an eye on the cat. 'He's half-monster and he's always going to be.'

'It's nothing to do with ye,' said May.

'Wrong,' said Theodora. 'I'm his cure. I can clear those things out of his body.'

The four cats on the roof stopped in their tracks. They sat and watched Theodora, their tales curling this way and that.

'Ye can?' asked May.

'Yeah,' said Theodora, 'I checked him out this morning. I can take Andrew's infection just like I take abilities from girls. I wouldn't want them for myself, they're nasty little critters. I'd just cast them off.'

'He's in the guest house,' May said slowly. 'Ye could go fix him right now.'

Already May knew that would not happen. On her chest she could feel the squeeze of a dreadful decision having to be made. The cats around Theodora lowered their heads and straightened their tails. They waited.

Grimly, Theodora leaned forwards on her knees. She was in a powerful position. She did not need to indulge in cruelty. In fact, she had genuine regret for May and her situation. She was sorry it had come to this. 'You know what you have to give me first,' she said.

The cats raised their furry heads and set to meowing loud and pitifully, like they were tortured or starving.

'Theodora!' exclaimed Mrs Honeyford. 'You've returned to us!' She was looking up from her front garden. Theodora crunched down with embarrassment, as if she had been trying to impress someone when a mollycoddling relative blundered in. 'How ever did you get up there?' Mrs Honeyford called to her. 'Come in for some dinner!'

Other villagers were approaching. Maybe they were looking for their cats. What they found was Theodora sitting on the Honeyfords' roof. She looked different, gaunt with a new severity around the eyes. But it was

146

definitely her. Theodora had never contacted anyone after running away. Not even her parents.

'Theodora's back!' gasped Mr Foster.

'We're so glad to see you!' Mr Merriman called up to her.

'Oh, the relief!' cried Betty Bird.

'I'm NOT back,' said Theodora. She hated the way they were all staring at her, all delighted and gooey. None of them had changed a bit.

The villagers gathered to see her, their prodigal daughter. May was among them but was hardly aware of what was happening. Her eyes were blank. Her knuckles were white. Theodora's proposition filled her every sense. Andrew could be healed but only in exchange for May's ability. It would mean becoming an ordinary girl.

Ordinary. Not special ever again.

'Please stay,' Mr Hume was calling to Theodora. 'It doesn't matter that you couldn't be a Bride of the Lake. Most of us probably couldn't. This is still home. You belong with us.'

'I've just made a batch of scones,' said Mrs Grace.

'And I'll make a big pot of tea,' said Mr Hopkins.

Theodora squirmed. She could not run because she was stuck on this roof. She could not fly because she did not want these people knowing she could. 'Just leave me alone,' she said.

147

It got worse. More villagers arrived. The man from the *Bugle* dashed from his office and started snapping photos of her. *Theodora Returns!* Such good news would deserve a two-page feature.

Theodora shrieked and covered her face.

Down the track came Farmer Able. He was bent over and walking crookedly. There was a reason for that. 'Give me my stick back, you whippersnapper!' he said.

'I'm just borrowing it,' yelled Theodora. 'Just leave me be a while.'

Stealing old men's walking sticks – the people of Lough Linger did not approve of thing like that.

'Great to have you back home,' said Mr Hume, 'but won't you please return Mr Able's stick?'

'I'm NOT BACK,' said Theodora. 'Leave me alone.'

But they could not leave her any more than they could have ignored a sick lamb. Loads of villagers were there, offering her things and asking her questions. Along the track came an '*eeek*'. It was a low-volume exclamation compared to everyone else's, yet it cut through and was heard by the whole crowd. They heard it because that *eeek* was packed with an intense amount of shock, joy, sorrow and disbelief. It had come from Theodora's mother. Both the Farrs had been out for a stroll.

Everybody looked but nobody spoke. Theodora had been gone three years. Her parents stood frozen.

The only sound was a *click* as the man from the *Bugle* took their picture.

'Who's that?' said Theodora, pointing. Her father was pushing a pram.

'This is your new brother,' he said. His throat dried up but that was nothing. For three years his throat had been dry, his eyes had been dry, he was an entirely dry husk. Since his daughter ran away, Thomas Farr had been a walking desert. Not even Lough Linger was enough to wet him, though he drank it by the gallon. It had taken their new baby to bring a flow back into his life. To bring peace.

'Well that's *lovely*,' said Theodora spitefully. 'Maybe this one won't be faulty, like me.'

Theodora was shaking and gripping hard on Farmer Able's stick. Her parents looked at one another. The villagers bowed their heads. The man from the *Bugle* lowered his camera.

'I'm done here anyway,' said Theodora, jumping to her feet. 'This was just a flying visit.' Then, to everyone's profound shock, she took off. She cruised twenty metres up the track while the villagers yelled and swooned. Theodora landed by the Hopkins' white picket fence, stared defiantly at everyone then threw the walking stick at Farmer Able's feet. 'Have it,' she said. Using both hands she seized one of the fence's verticals and pulled it away, nails and all. Its base would not break so easily so she kicked at it, once, twice, three times. Her face was bright red. Her silvery hair whipped. Finally the wood snapped and she had it, a plank the size of a skateboard. She threw it down and stood on it. She kicked off and was high in the air.

'Think about it!' she shouted as she left them all behind.

The villagers would indeed think about what they had just seen. Only May knew that Theodora's last words were actually meant for her. She had been offered a deal.

Heal Andrew but become an ordinary girl.

Ordinary. Not special ever again.

17

Ewan was at the kitchen table in Amber Feather's cottage. A vase of flowers stood in the middle of the table among heaps of vegetables and fruit. Amber pushed a bowl of green apples across the tabletop towards him. They were as shiny as the 'go' on traffic lights.

'I am not eating anything that grew here,' he said.

Amber watched him patiently. 'Was it Mr Swift who told you about our tradition?' she asked.

'Why would he?' said Ewan. 'He's in on it too, isn't he? You're all in on it.'

'Yes,' Amber sighed at the boy's phrasing, 'we're all *in on it.*'

'Mr Swift didn't tell me anything,' said Ewan. 'Someone else did and I am not saying who. Then *logic* told me that the creature is no angel. You've such easy lives.' Ewan indicated the tabletop of food and the comfy home. 'Something must get sacrificed for it. Or in this case *someone.*'

151

'You're honourable and clever,' said Amber. 'I knew you were special from the day you arrived.'

That infuriated Ewan. 'Stop the flattery!' he said. 'I am never falling for that again.'

'But it's true,' insisted Amber. 'And I'm not the only one who thinks so. We all do. That's why I'm now formally inviting you to stay with us as long as you like. To become a citizen of Lough Linger.'

Ewan was halted by the proposition. Yesterday he would have done anything for such an offer.

'Become a citizen of Lough Linger,' said Ewan, his voice low and angry, 'and help you feed that monster?'

Amber got annoyed. She straightened in her chair. 'I won't have you talk about Uncle like that,' she said.

She went to a pile of cardboard boxes stacked behind a door. She pulled them down and rummaged through them. They were full of documents. She lifted out piles of papers and stacked them here and there. Or just threw sheets over her shoulder as she dug. A mess grew around her. Paper stacks got knocked and slid apart, fanning pages over the floorboards or sending them gliding through the air. At last she found one brown page and sat up to read from it.

'Listen to this,' she said, 'it's from 1790. "The blacksmith Toby Melody was resting on the far shore when Uncle did reveal itself. Tears came to the blacksmith's eyes at the charm of our guardian's countenance. Uncle reached forth and with an enormous but delicate finger wiped the tears from his cheek. Then Uncle slipped back under the lake, having said not a word and leaving no ripple." Now, does that sound like a monster?'

'No,' said Ewan, 'but it sounds like a lie.'

'We don't lie in Lough Linger,' said Amber.

'*Nothing unusual* in the lake, you told me,' said Ewan.

'Uncle is not unusual to us,' she said. 'Look, there's a picture.'

On the back of the page someone had drawn a giant figure with wings, peeking innocently from the water.

Ewan made an unimpressed noise and looked away.

Amber got up and went to sit opposite the boy. She looked at him, openly seeking a way to win him over. 'Ever considered joining the army?' she asked.

'No.'

Amber crunched into an apple and chewed thoughtfully, gazing at Ewan. He looked out of the window. Everything was changed to him now. The lake was calm yet treacherous. Those bizarre brothers were still fishing from the jetty. Children were playing marbles in the shade of the sacrifice vessel, the *Bridal Sweet*.

'You wouldn't blame someone for joining the armed forces though, would you?' said Amber. 'That would be their right, right?'

'People can do what they want,' said Ewan. He flashed her a look. 'Within reason.'

Amber nibbled at her apple. 'Sure. Now please have a fruit, you haven't eaten all day.'

Ewan looked away out of the window again.

'The Brides volunteer,' Amber said after a while.

'They're brainwashed,' said Ewan. 'Growing up here gives them twisted ideas.'

'No more than any other place,' said Amber. 'They go to Uncle in full knowledge of what they're doing. They volunteer to do it because they know it's for the greater good. Just like a soldier.'

So that was her angle. Ewan scoffed. 'A soldier has a chance of coming home from a war,' he said.

'But they're prepared to give their lives and many do,' countered Amber. 'Also, the Brides of the Lake can change their minds anytime, right up to the moment the boat is pushed out. Soldiers cannot. *Plus* we treat the Brides of the Lake far better than any nation treats its soldiers, not only during their lives with us but after they've gone to Uncle too. Every crop we harvest, every tree we chop, every time we say good morning, everything we do honours their memory. Here kids grow up knowing the debt they owe the Brides. Call it brainwashing if you like but I call it *grateful*. Some of them, just some of them, choose to follow their example.'

Through the window Ewan watched the children

on the jetty. Most were concentrating on their game but one little boy was standing apart and staring over the lake. A future Bride perhaps? Was he feeling the call of duty?

'You're an educated lad, you'll have options,' said Amber. 'It's boys with fewer options who often fill the ranks of armies. When their country is threatened they are sent to deal with it. Every nation with an army is prepared to do the same thing – sacrifice a small number of young citizens to protect the majority. Lough Linger is the same. At least here every child is free to choose. Maybe you can't agree that we're any better than a big nation but I refuse to believe that we're any worse.'

Ewan said nothing. He could not come up with a counter argument at that moment.

'Won't you at least have an apple?' asked Amber, proffering the bowl again.

Ewan took one and bit. It was something to do while thinking about soldiers and the sacrificed and whether they were similar or not.

Amber went back to rummaging through the files. Ewan sat quietly, eating the apple. Eventually Amber found what she was after, a crinkly old certificate. She sat back down opposite Ewan.

'And you have a home here if you want it,' she said. 'Far from Social Services and the police. Far from any trouble. For a few years or forever, nobody will be able to take it away from you.'

Amber put the certificate on top of the apples. It had a wax seal and flourished handwriting. 'The title deeds to the guest house,' she explained. 'It gives you ownership if you sign it. Put your name on the deeds and the house is yours. Go now and think about it.'

Ewan stood up. He meant to look at the deeds but his gaze got stuck on the flowers in the vase.

'You're thinking of Brigit, aren't you?' said Amber.

'Might be,' he said.

'Ewan, she has *chosen*. She might be the only person to go to Uncle this year. In the outside world hundreds of people die too young every day. Hundreds of boys and girls, in war or from disease. Maybe our tradition is not perfect. But it's the best possible deal that can be made between life and death.'

Ewan left Amber's cottage. The children who had been playing marbles on the jetty ran past him, laughing. The little boy had rejoined them and was laughing too. The lake lay motionless. Dogs were sleeping in doorways. He dragged his feet through the peaceful village. He found Andrew sitting in a cabbage patch near the guest house and brought him inside. Now it was May's turn to be missing. She had left Andrew alone so, wherever she was, it must be important. Ewan sat on the couch, under the heavy roof beams and between the thick walls. Homely, he used to call it.

18

Could May stand being an ordinary girl? What would she do then, go back to her hometown and live with her dad? After encountering Theodora she sat forwards on the guest house couch with her face in her hands and was motionless for a whole hour. Andrew detected grief and had stayed next to her, faithful and quiet. When May raised her face she knew what she had to do. She had to go see her dad. It was not advice she needed. She just had to see him.

'I'm sorry, ye have to look out for yourself a wee while,' she had said to Andrew, patting his hands.

May walked out of the valley and into the rain. She walked for hours more. The ground was sodden. Cars raced along distant roads. She stumbled upon a fly-tip. A refrigerator, old armchairs and mattresses were strewn about and slowly turning brown. This was the real world. Animals kept low, they were wary and survivalist, but May found enough assistance to locate her dad's campsite. But when she got there he was gone. Nothing left but a square of flattened grass and a black circle where a campfire had been.

Man moved on, she received.

It was coming from an owl huddled in a cranny in a high cliff. His eyesight was failing and his skull was congested but he knew the country and knew where the stranger had moved to, chased off by a farmer for trespass. In May's mind the owl took her by the wrist and pointed her in the right direction. May began to walk but stopped. She looked up at the cliff.

'Is it true that owls got wisdom?' she said out loud but inside too.

It was a long time before something like an answer took shape between May's ears. *If I was smart I could catch a mouse. Instead I am hungry.*

'That's terrible,' said May. She pointed the owl's attention towards the stone hills around Lough Linger.

'Go live there,' she said, 'they've got it easy.'

The bird was only further wearied by the suggestion. Creakily, he stretched out one wing then the other. *Do not trust that place*, May received from him. *It feels wrong.*

'Ha!' said May. *Ye are wise.*

Wise but hungry.

What about me dad? May wondered. *Do ye think I can trust him?*

You can trust him to be him, considered the owl, *but that does not mean he will be good for you. He is unable to take the weight of this life. Perhaps he wants you to carry his load for him.*

So I can't trust where I've been, thought May, *and can't trust where I'm goin'. Anything I can trust?*

Not much, reckoned the owl, *but we do not need a lot to thrive. Find a strong ledge and stick to it.*

Me friends are good ledges, May thought and she smiled. But the next thought was painful. *I've a friend and I can break him from this awful prison he's in. But it means ye might be the last animal I ever commune with.*

May received no reaction. She waited. The owl did not seem to understand the seriousness of May's situation. It was like he was waiting for her to get to the point. In the mountains things died all the time. What was it for one creature to lose her voice? Very little.

My finest communion is a mouse snapping in my beak, considered the owl. *The mouse too, I know, will have had its fine moments. All we mountain creatures have one thing in common. We never feel sorry for ourselves. I will fall dead from this ledge some night without ever having self-pitied. Only humans and dogs feel sorry for themselves.*

May sighed. 'That's the last time I go crying to an owl,' she said.

A cheerful rap on the guest house door was accompanied by a cheerful call. 'Hello, just visiting!'

159

Ewan leaped from the couch and retreated to the bedroom. Andrew watched Ewan hide and scratched his head with his mighty paw. Mr Swift let himself in. He stood on the welcome mat and smiled at Andrew. 'Anybody else home?' he called.

Andrew grunted at the door Ewan was hiding behind but Ewan did not reveal himself.

Mr Swift's eyes roved about as he waited for a response. None came and he was pleased. 'Shall we take a walk?' he said to Andrew, making a walking sign with his fingers. Andrew got the message and rose to his feet. 'Good, good,' said Mr Swift. 'Let's leave by the back door.'

The guest house was at the back of the village so it was easy for Mr Swift to lead Andrew away without being seen by anyone. They went into a plantation. As he walked Mr Swift used his cane to hold twigs away from his face. Andrew blundered along behind, snapping branches and shouldering trunks so hard their tops shook. Ahead, small animals dashed from their path.

'Anywhere else pines would need years to grow this big,' Mr Swift explained, 'but here, fed by Lough Linger, they grow as fast as flowers. The fecundity of the place!'

Andrew did not understand a word but made vocal sounds at the appropriate times. Mr Swift, in a good-tempered manner, treated this as conversation. From a distance it sounded like they were actually chatting. 'I enjoy your company a great deal, young man,' Mr Swift said to Andrew at one point. 'I can really talk to you.'

They made their way deep into the woods.

'I was glad to see your antagonism towards the Lesser-Spotted Blossom,' said Mr Swift. 'It's the abominable fruit of that lake. But still just a plant. What might you make of the living, breathing creature in the lake? I've created a manikin to help us find out. I hope you'll find it agreeable. Or rather, utterly *disagreeable*.'

Mr Swift stopped in a circular clearing in the pines. Tired by the walk, he leaned against a tree. He pulled a hip flask from his pocket and drained it. Anywhere else such a flask would have contained whiskey or brandy, but this was Lough Linger.

'Lake water,' Mr Swift explained, raising the hip flask. 'Leaves a bad taste in my mouth but I must live, mustn't I? Until my work is done.'

Andrew was focused on the large lump of wood in the middle of the clearing. He crooked his head, trying to understand it. It was the size of a chair, roughly hewn from a log and painted blue. It was in the shape of a human hand, reaching up.

Close by, a mechanism of pulleys and ropes was bolted to a tree. Mr Swift was pulling a few pegs from it, priming the device. Ropes ran from it and Andrew's eyes followed them. Some shot away into the upper branches. Others ran to ground and disappeared under the pine needles. A calculating gurgle rolled in Andrew's throat as he studied the ground. The ropes could be snaking anywhere under there but probably to the blue hand. Andrew's brain was crude with most things but sharp on tactics and battlefields. His blackened blood was already warming up.

Mr Swift sat in the wooden hand. He used a couple of leather belts as a harness, strapping himself in. Andrew growled. 'That's right, young man!' said Mr Swift. 'There's something afoot!'

Mr Swift held his cane by the tip and brought it back and forth a couple of times, taking aim. It was let fly. The cane arrowed out of the clearing and struck its target with a *bing*. It was a round bin lid nailed to a plank. The plank was hinged and creaked away. This caused a weight, a bottle full of stones, to drop. A rope tensed then strained. Somewhere high in the treetops a peg was pulled, shooting into the air like a champagne cork. Another weight dropped, a sack of stones this time. Ropes whipped and came alive. Mr Swift looked at Andrew, grinned, and said, 'Help me.'

He took off.

Ropes twanged. The ground opened. The blue hand was just the tip of Mr Swift's project. A wooden arm emerged, holding up the hand, smelling of paint and dirt. Then a head burst up through the loose soil, then shoulders. Mr Swift was elevated to greater and greater heights. The pines around the clearing bent inwards as they took the strain, the massive puppet dangling from a dozen ropes. Its torso emerged, left arm and legs. Chain links had been hammered in to work as joints, connecting each limb. The wood of the arms and legs were hardly carved at all, they were just trunks painted blue. But Mr Swift had put plenty of effort into sculpting the head. It had wicked eyes and zigzag teeth locked in an evil grin. This was Mr Swift's opinion of the giant in the lake.

'Help me! Help me!' Mr Swift was shouting, enjoying his role as a helpless victim in the giant's grip. He was way up in the air.

Andrew did not compute that this was a fake display. His bones angled and locked, asserting his muscles against his skin and stretching it to breaking point. His adrenalin surged. His hair stood on end. His eyes bulged.

Dangling fully out of the ground, the puppet's secondary mechanisms came into play. Its left arm swung like a boat's boom. Andrew saw it rapidly filling the corner of his eye. He leaped straight upwards.

Whiiiisssssh. The arm swept beneath him.

Andrew hit the ground in an attack-ready crouch. Another weight dropped behind the puppet and Mr Swift's last touch was revealed. Uncle's wings were made from doors and also painted blue. They swung both ways from behind its back and clunked into position. And there it was, complete. Uncle, a cruel angel.

Monster = Bad.

The left arm returned to take another swipe at Andrew. Again Andrew jumped but this time on top of it. The arm reeled as his feet slammed down. Andrew used it as a launch pad, leaping higher. In the air he was face to face with the puppet. Andrew bared his teeth at the giant's grin. The monster-boy, so awkward in normal circumstances, was like lightning in war. Flipping in the air, Andrew kicked Uncle in the chest. Its arms waved as it took the blow. A support rope snapped. The whole puppet jigged.

'Good kick, sir!' shouted Mr Swift.

Andrew twirled twice as he returned to ground.

BAM.

Every pine needle in the clearing bounced as he landed. Andrew was only grounded a split second before launching again. He slotted a foot in at the giant's waist and launched higher. He grabbed its blue shoulder in one hand. He did not like the way the giant was grinning at him. Andrew retracted his other hand and made into a fist.

He punched the puppet's head clean off.

The head flew through the trees and hit the ground like a comet, ploughing a channel through the soil and only stopping when it struck the base of a tree. This happened to be the tree Ewan was hiding behind. He had followed them from the guest house. He could see that Amber was right to be suspicious of the teacher. Mr Swift certainly had taken against their community. He planned to attack its very heart, using Andrew.

Ewan peeked around at the wooden head. It grinned back up at him.

'Help me!' Mr Swift was shouting to Andrew.

This time he meant it.

Ropes were whipping wild. With its head gone and supports snapped, the puppet's centre of gravity was crashing around. Andrew clamped his knees to the monster's shoulders, locked like a cowboy on a bucking bronco. Andrew lunged for the arm holding up Mr Swift, slamming both palms against the wood. His fingers wedged in solidly. Fibres rent apart. Sap squirted. The arm gave up. Andrew squeezed his thumbs and forefingers together straight through the log. It exploded in a loud pop and a cloud of sawdust.

Mr Swift dropped. 'WAAHH!'

The old man sprang in the air, staying up. The hand he was harnessed to was still suspended from above by two ropes. But pulverising the arm had set loose other parts. The puppet slumped to one side and turned, tangling itself in rope. The wings were lassoed and forced back to pre-launch position. Its left arm became lashed to its legs. Andrew just rode with the collapsing monster, astride its torso. The pines were bending harder and closer, blocking out the sky. Their tops crossed each other, stripping each other's branches. It rained bark and pine needles as the trees formed a dome. Had Andrew reached up he could have touched the top. The wood creaked then squealed.

Then stopped.

Mr Swift resisted yelling.

Silence . . .

Almost.

A fine *hummmmmm* remained. It was the sound of ropes and tree trunks stretched to their limit and pinned in high tension. Mr Swift and Andrew looked over at each other. Spring-loaded energy was tensed all around them. They could feel the air vibrate against their skin. The super-taut ropes, the bent trees, the whole twisted mess was like a mousetrap, a breath away from snapping. And they were in the middle of it.

Humm—

The trap went off.

It was Andrew who set it off. He dived for Mr Swift, putting slam in his dive, grabbing the harness and ripping the old man away from the wooden hand. Mr Swift was separated from his puppet and this was good because in the same second the trees unbent at one hundred kilometres an hour. Every rope whiplashed. The puppet was torn limb from limb. The torso was catapulted straight upwards, taking fifteen metres of rope with it. *Swisssssssh*. Two seconds later it was a tiny black dot in the sky. A wing was flung away over the plantation. Catching the wind it would fly clear out of the valley, glide under rain-clouds and eventually bury itself in a bog. The puppet's left arm was fired in the other direction. It rocketed, unnoticed, over the village and into Lough Linger. It hit the lake bottom and splintered.

What the real Uncle might have made of this painted log can only be guessed at.

Andrew hit the ground standing, taking the recoil in his knees. He looked at the destruction he had wrought. Chunks of the dead monster were lying on the ground or swinging in the branches. He made a satisfied shake with his shoulders.

'Astounding,' said Mr Swift. Andrew grunted and looked up. His bigger hand was raised in the air, just like the puppet's had been, and was gripping Mr Swift by his harness. The teacher hardly seemed aware of how he was dangling off the ground. He was awe-struck by Andrew's heroic strength and agility.

'Astounding,' Mr Swift said again.

Andrew put him down. His breathing slowed. His bones crackled as they resettled.

'Astounding.' Fiery light danced in Mr Swift's eyes while he admired the destruction.

A high whistle was approaching, fast. It was coming at them from the sky. The sound was at a pitch Mr Swift's ears could not detect. But Andrew heard it. He grabbed the old man and pulled him to the clearing's edge.

The torso was back.

It crashed to earth. The trees shook. Soil gushed into the air. The puppet's torso had been launched into such a perfect vertical that, after shooting a kilometre straight up, it had fallen back to exactly the same spot and buried itself into the clearing.

Mr Swift slumped back against a tree, suddenly feeling his age. 'Absolutely astounding,' he whispered. He stared at the pit then turned to Andrew. 'So many years I've waited,' he said, 'and at last you have come.' Mr Swift began to sob, tears rolling down his cheeks. 'All this time I was waiting for you. You, a hero who will free us. You, a scourge of monsters. You, a champion. You ... it was you I was waiting for. You will kill Uncle.'

19

It was midnight. May had still not returned but that was not unusual, she could wander off for days at a time. Her absence suited Ewan. It would be tough for him to explain what he was about to do. It had taken hours just to persuade himself.

Andrew was snoring on the guest-house floor. Ewan paused and looked at him before leaving. 'I am sorry,' he said to the sleeping monster-boy. 'I don't know if I am doing the right thing, or the smart thing, or just something selfish.'

He went and knocked on Amber's door.

'Ewan, it's late,' she said, 'are you all right?'

'I want to stay in Lough Linger,' he said.

Amber smiled. 'That's a good decision.'

'Mr Swift *is* plotting against the community,' said Ewan. 'I can get the evidence you need.'

Amber took a deep breath. 'Come in.'

Ewan strode in before he changed his mind. He went straight for the kitchen. The title deeds certificate was still resting on the bowl of apples. The flowers were gone. Just as well, they could be distracting.

'I almost just woke Andrew and left with him,' he said. 'I don't know who's worse, Mr Swift or Uncle. I don't know if Brigit should be allowed to sacrifice herself. I don't know anything anymore. May is right. This place is not natural.'

'Natural or not,' said Amber, 'I'll never leave. It's my home. And that's what we all need, isn't it? A home.'

'I guess so,' said Ewan.

'And now you have one.'

There was a pause until Ewan said, 'Mr Swift is going to use Andrew to attack Uncle.'

Amber was not surprised. 'I'm sorry I didn't tell you all my fears from the beginning,' she said, 'but that's what I suspected Mr Swift might be planning.' She looked out of her window. Ewan followed her eyes. A lantern was lighting the end of the jetty and the brothers Earlly were still fishing. Amber explained, 'Mr Swift would need a boat to bring Andrew out and the *Bridal Sweet* is the only one in the village. I asked the Earlly boys to pull it up and keep guard over it day and night.'

'So that's why they're always there,' said Ewan. 'To protect Uncle.'

'No,' said Amber firmly. 'To protect Andrew. Swift is a fool, he really is. Andrew would not stand a chance against Uncle.'

Ewan remembered how Andrew had demolished the puppet. 'Are you sure?' he asked.

'Uncle is humble and a peace lover,' she said. 'But it has lived thousands of years and I'm sure it can defend itself. If Andrew picks a fight with Uncle it is Andrew who will lose, that's definite. That's why you mustn't worry about reporting Mr Swift. You're saving Andrew's life.'

The gravity of the situation suddenly hit Ewan. He had to sit down. Amber closed the blinds and put on the kettle for tea. Ewan ate an apple. He had not eaten since the last one.

Amber poured the tea and said, 'So, you mentioned evidence?'

Next morning Mrs Honeyford got out her watercolours. Mrs Foster opened her tea shop and put a special offer on fairy cakes. Mr Merriman drank a pint of lake water. They were nothing if not consistent. Every day of their lives had been agreeable and pleasant. They assumed today was going to be like any other. They were wrong.

Word spread through the village. It was spread thoroughly, right to the corners, like the butter on morning toast. The villagers tried to absorb it. They hushed and retreated behind closed doors. Closed doors were an unusual sight in Lough Linger. The sound of crying came from Miss Boswell's front room.

No one called across the fields. No one leaned on their gates. The cats could not settle in their usual sunny spots. Even they knew something was wrong.

One of the young visitors had gone to the Mayor and claimed that Mr Swift was plotting against Uncle. He said he had proof.

School was cancelled. Shops and the sawmill stayed shut. Crops were left untended. Gradually people came out and gathered before the community centre, shaking their heads and whispering. Only Mr Swift stayed away. Amber Feather stood outside the double doors. She was keeping Ewan by her side and requiring him to confirm publicly what he had witnessed.

'Mr Swift was going to use Andrew,' said Ewan for the umpteenth time, his head down.

'Speak up,' said Amber, 'everyone has to hear you.'

Ewan raised his chin a fraction. 'Mr Swift was going to use Andrew to try and kill Uncle,' he said.

Villagers were struck cold. Their own dear Mr Swift? Attack their guardian, their protector, the source of all that was good, that beautiful blue-skinned angel, Uncle? It was the worst thing they had ever heard. This was the worst day they had ever seen. Some were so shaken they had to sit down right there in the dust of the track.

'Maybe you ate too many sugary things?' suggested Miss Boswell, her eyes still red. 'Might your imagination have gotten overstimulated?'

Ewan shook his head stiffly. He was not comfortable in his role as spy. 'Here's your evidence coming,' he said, relieved something else could now speak for him.

Thomas Farr was leading a troop of sawmill workers back from a plantation. The Mayor had sent them off earlier with a stretcher, a tarpaulin tied between two long poles. In it they were now carrying something large and heavy. The villagers let them through. When they dropped the load the tarpaulin fell open and a wooden head was revealed. In one impulse every villager leaped back. Hands went to mouths, shocked. The puppet's blue head grinned its sleazy grin at them all.

'See!' said Amber Feather. It was undiplomatic but she could not suppress a victorious tone. 'This is what Mr Swift thinks of Uncle. We have no option. He must be exiled.'

Again villagers expressed themselves as one. 'Noooo,' they moaned. At his age, forcing Mr Swift from the valley was a death sentence.

'Exactly what he tried to force on many of you,' Amber argued. 'Uncle keeps the water good and that's what keeps you alive.'

Some villagers began weeping. They wrapped their arms around their heads, unable to absorb the horror of it all.

Mr Hume's study of philosophy helped him stay

reasonable and balanced. 'We are grateful to our guest for defending Uncle,' he said, stroking his white beard, 'but now Mr Swift must be allowed the chance to defend himself.'

'That's right! Of course!' Villagers grabbed the idea and clung to it. Mr Swift must be allowed to reply to Ewan and his evidence. They all agreed it should be so. At the very least it would put off the moment when they might have to make a harsh judgement against a friend and neighbour.

'Innocent until proven guilty!' said Mr Foster, quoting something people said on the telly. The villagers knew little of courts or legal processes but agreed that the teacher should have the chance to give his side of the story. It was decided to put Mr Swift on trial. The case would be heard that night, in the community centre. There had never been a trial in Lough Linger before. People gulped at the thought. They went home to tidy things that were already tidy.

Ewan used the chance to get away from Amber's side. He wanted to be alone. But villagers were everywhere. They gave him weak smiles, consoling looks, offers of tea and sandwiches.

'Don't worry,' Mrs Merriman said to Ewan, seeing his discomfort at what might happen to Mr Swift. 'Our trial won't be like those trials we see on television. There'll be no shouting or unpleasantness.'

'Certainly not,' agreed Carrick McCuddy. 'It'll be a *nice* trial.'

Ewan hurried away. No trial could be nice when the sentence was exile, then death.

'I'll make a batch of scones,' Mrs Grace called after him.

'And I'll make us a big pot of tea,' added Mr Hopkins.

Ewan had not escaped yet. His entire class from school were waiting up by the guest house, about twenty sets of bleached cuffs, polished teeth and bright eyes. They looked at him steadily, as if trying to read something in his face. Steadiest of all was Brigit.

'You have chosen your side,' she said.

'Seems so,' said Ewan.

'It grieves us to think of Mr Swift so troubled all these years,' said Brigit.

The class mumbled agreement. Many were tearful. A depression hung over the Honeyford boys. The students were amazed that Ewan, a boy their age, could have detected Mr Swift's hidden malice. And been cunning enough to snare him. None of them could have done such things. They were amazed but disturbed too.

'It's the quiet ones you've got to watch,' said Ewan.

Ewan's remark only saddened Brigit further. 'Mr Swift was not what we would have called *quiet*,' she said. 'On the contrary, he talked a lot and was always cheerful. That's why it's shocking to discover he was tormented and warped on the inside. To plot the death of Uncle! It's not an easy thing to forgive.'

The students looked to the lake, seeking the strength to forgive their teacher.

Brigit had already risen to the challenge. She looked at Ewan with a stoic smile. 'But I've done it,' she said, placing her hand over her heart. 'I have forgiven him.'

He did not let it show but Ewan was suddenly angry. 'That's generous of you,' he said.

'Oh no,' said Brigit. 'Not *generous*. Necessary. One must do these things for one's soul.'

The mention of souls prompted the students to lower their heads solemnly. Ewan hated this atmosphere. Had he been alone with Brigit he might have let rip. Forgiving might be hard but was often easier than thinking. Brigit forgave Mr Swift so she would not have to think about his actions. She forgave him instead of trying to understand him. *At least Mr Swift is able to think freely. At least Mr Swift has his own mind.* Ewan thought those things. But what he said was, 'How is your soul, Brigit?'

She lowered her head in humility. 'I am told it is good enough,' she said.

Another student stepped forward. 'We've come here to tell you how grateful we are,' she said. 'Grateful that you've exposed Mr Swift's wicked plan and made sure no harm comes to Uncle.'

'Or to Andrew for that matter,' added another student.

'Yes, thank you,' said another.

Each student thanked him. Ewan absorbed their appreciation and resisted the urge to run away screaming.

Their thanks given, students began to drift off. Brigit delayed. 'When you came to my room you were against my going to the lake,' she said and waited for him to respond.

'You're entitled to do what you want,' said Ewan.

'Wonderful,' said Brigit. 'You finally understand how much I want to go to Uncle.' Ewan turned away but looked back again when she spoke with something like weakness in her voice. 'Tonight at the trial,' said Brigit, 'when you are testifying against Mr Swift, may I pretend you're doing it for me? Even just a little?'

Never before had Ewan heard Brigit *wanting* – wanting something that she might not be allowed. For once she seemed helpless. Ewan's heart rate spiked. All anger left him. He wanted so badly to touch her hand that he actually saw himself doing it. Saw Brigit's pale fingers entwine with his.

But in reality he had not moved.

'You won't have to pretend,' said Ewan. 'I will be doing it for you.'

Brigit blinked. Nobody said anything. She went to

leave with the others but stopped for one last thing. 'Will you permit me to give you this token?' she asked Ewan. She removed a flower from her hair and offered it to him.

Ewan went inside, holding the flower in his cupped hands. He was not sure what to do with it. In the kitchen was a large heavy cookbook. Ewan opened it in the middle and pressed the flower between its pages.

20

Mr Swift stood at his mirror. The lines on his face disappeared as evening faded to dark. He buttoned up his waistcoat, drawing in his stomach to make the last button. He liked the feeling of tightness around him. It made him feel alert. Mr Swift stood straighter than he had in years. He stayed at the mirror, studying what he had become. In ten minutes his trial would begin. Mr Swift put on his favourite bow tie. This was a special occasion.

That Mr Swift always lived alone made him peculiar in Lough Linger. Everyone else paired up as naturally as swallows. Farmer Able lived alone too but that was different, he was a widow. He had a wife once. They had been married for one hundred and thirty years.

Most believed an ideal partner for everyone was another of Uncle's blessings. You did not have to leave the valley. There was someone for everyone right here. For decades it was nudged and whispered that Mr Swift and Miss Boswell ought to marry. They always danced together at community fetes. She laughed at his jokes.

But no, no. It could not be.

Mr Swift lived for one thing and one thing only. Every day he forced lake water between his teeth in the hope of seeing, some day, Uncle's corpse floating on the surface of Lough Linger. Their tradition was wrong. Their lives were too long. But it was one bitter loss that kept Mr Swift burning – what would his life have been like if he had spent it with Molly? Infinitely better, fuller, brighter. Uncle had robbed him.

Mr Swift opened his dictionary on the table. He held his breath and delicately lifted the pressed dry flower onto one palm. All its pigment was gone. The lines of his hand were visible through its transparent edges. He lifted the flower to his face, close to his lips as if about to kiss it. But he did not. Eyes closed, he blew on to it. The flower disintegrated into thousands of pieces. Each flake lifted into the air, making a cloud that slowly dispersed. When Mr Swift opened his eyes his hand was empty.

There was a bang on the door.

It was time.

Mr Swift took his cane from its hook and gave a last glance at the old face in the mirror. There had been enough years already. So many spent just waiting, just passing the time. The last few days had been more significant than the last few decades. The next hour would be the most important of all.

The brothers Earlly were standing outside the door. 'Amber sent us to fetch you,' said the first. He wanted to sound gruff but did not quite manage it. This was due to inexperience, it was the first time he had tried to sound gruff in his entire life. Mr Swift went with them.

'An escort was hardly necessary,' he said. 'I know the way to the community centre.'

The second brother was watching Mr Swift with a perplexed look on his face, like a child just learning things are sometimes unfair or plain weird. 'Don't you know what losing Uncle would mean to people our age?' he asked.

'Stiff knees?' suggested Mr Swift.

It was a small village. They were already at the community centre. Uncle's wooden head was gone. How to be rid of it was a subject of concern much of the day. The idea of burning it had made everyone uneasy. It seemed sacrilegious. In the end it was buried in a grave.

Inside the community centre were rows of chairs, each one holding a citizen. They faced the front, the perfect boy in the stained glass window looking over them. Mr Swift could have named each villager by the shapes of their ears and the particular hunches they had when self-conscious, as they were now. No one turned to look at Mr Swift but he knew it was not because they were angry. It was because they found the whole situation painful. Everyone, apart from the visitors, would vote on Mr Swift's guilt or innocence. Even children. The whole community would be judge and jury. Mr Swift walked the aisle. His cane tapped against the floor and chairs creaked, right and left, as the people he passed shifted uncomfortably. Amber Feather stood by the podium and watched him all the way. He sat down on the front row. The brothers Earlly sat either side, an unnecessary touch. Neither Andrew nor May were present. But Ewan was.

Amber took to walking slowly back and forth, building up to the trial. An atmosphere of confrontation thickened in the air. People breathed it in and felt ill. 'Will Ewan please take the podium,' she said, 'and tell us what he witnessed in the plantation.'

Ewan stood too quickly. He was sure everyone could hear his heart beating. He got up on the podium and gripped its sides with his clammy hands. Seeing all Lough Linger's faces arranged in rows made it striking just how many of them were old. A lot of grey heads were looking back at him. A lot of wrinkly eyes. Ewan hated having to give evidence against Mr Swift. Every moment was agony. When he opened his mouth to speak Mr Swift put him out of his misery.

'No need for that,' said the teacher, his voice projecting throughout the community centre. 'We already know what he says he saw and heard. And it's all true. I admit it.'

From the crowd came sighs, groans and tears. With a tilt of her head Amber dismissed Ewan. He kept his head bowed as he walked towards the double doors, feeling everyone's eyes on him. Even the eyes of the boy in the window, burning into his back. By the last few metres Ewan was almost running.

Mr Swift took the podium. He hung his cane on the side and straightened his bow tie. When he was ready Amber Feather turned on her heels towards him. She was determined to not waste a word during this exchange. Everything would be tight and streamlined. Swift be damned. She would be lean, she would be mean, a prosecuting machine. 'You admit planning an attack on Uncle?' she demanded.

'I did not think of it as attack. More like justice.'

Amber Feather revolved to face the villagers but directed her words to Mr Swift. 'Justice? Hardly. I put this to you: you were driven by bitterness and revenge. You wished to kill our guardian for the selfish reason that once, many years ago, a certain girl chose Uncle instead of you.'

'I've had long years to consider my motivation,' responded Mr Swift. Even if he was driven by revenge, he was not going to admit it now. Mr Swift would try to make a clean and logical case about right and wrong. 'It's not just about Molly. It's about who we are, about our humanity. What are citizens of Lough Linger? What are we really? I'll tell you what. We are the spineless servants of a monster. It is a generous master, I agree, but we are nothing more than its slaves.'

'You might as well argue that we are slaves to gravity because we stay on the ground, slaves to air because we breathe,' said Amber. 'Uncle is at the root of our lives. The rest of the world is mired in sorrow. They eat until they are fat. They pollute until they have poisoned themselves. They spend their lives squabbling until, one day, they drop dead of disease. Not here. Uncle has given us peace and plenty. And you want to throw that back in its face, for what? Because you want to make us free to *suffer*?'

'There is still suffering here,' said Mr Swift. 'The Brides of the Lake suffer as Uncle digests them.'

The audience gagged at the harsh language. It was unheard of.

Amber turned and stepped closer to the podium. 'A few choose, *choose* to go to Uncle,' she said. 'We've seen no evidence that they suffer hardship. Their union with Uncle is an occasion of joy.'

'It must be the deepest form of slavery,' said Mr Swift, 'when you believe your master's needs are also your own. When you are prepared to feed him your own children. This must end. I want the young people made free.'

'And what of the old people?' asked Amber.

Mr Swift paused before saying, 'We would be better off dead.'

The audience heaved, emitting a group sigh that rolled like a wave. Out of that wave Brigit stood and faced Mr Swift. Everyone fell silent. Amber Feather stepped aside respectfully.

'I am the next to go to Uncle,' said Brigit. 'We have certain words we use when talking about our tradition. We say the Brides *unite* with Uncle. We say the Brides *live on* in the lake. But I have a mind of my own, Mr Swift, please do not think I am a victim. I realise that my life will be short so that others' can be long. But, please believe me, Mr Swift, I go gladly. It is the meaning I want to give to my life. I will do it for my family. I will do it for my neighbours. I will do it even for you.'

She sat down again. A few rows back her parents gripped each other's hands. Their daughter had not looked at them but that was okay, they were used to that. Being a Bride was a singular position. Her parents were more than proud, they were stunned that they could have produced such a visionary child.

Mr Swift replied to Brigit with a quiet intensity. 'Old people should do what is right for the young, not the other way around,' he said. 'And, Brigit, you should experience the world, the common, crude, risky world, rather than die without having seen it. But if you refuse to look, if you insist on dying in this day-dream, then I will bring that world here to you. I will flood this valley with it.'

A hush fell over the community centre. Amber broke it, 'You hoped to,' she corrected him, 'but you've failed, thanks to Ewan.'

Mr Swift closed his eyes and slowly shook his head. He did not stop for a full twenty seconds. Everyone waited for him to finish.

'Miss Feather, you don't understand what you *really* did when you told Ewan not to trust me,' said Mr Swift. 'That boy knows a crime when he sees it. All you did was tell him he was not alone in feeling that way. You told him that he might have an ally in this village. Someone to help him save Brigit, someone to help him save all the Brides. I didn't know he was following us when I took Andrew into the plantation. But as soon as Ewan was certain of my ambition to kill Uncle he came out of his hiding place. I was shocked as you can imagine. Andrew had just proven himself a champion and I was so happy I was crying like a baby. But Ewan and I talked. We talked for hours.'

Amber's arms dropped by her sides.

'We made a plan,' Mr Swift was saying, smiling now. 'I would talk to the community . . .'

The ground wobbled beneath Amber's feet as she felt, for the first time, the manipulation that was working her.

'And while I was doing that,' Mr Swift went on, 'Ewan would bring Andrew out on the lake to kill Uncle.'

Dozens of chair legs scraped the floor as a ripple of realisation ran through the crowd. The brothers Eartly looked at each other. Where was Ewan? Where was Andrew? Who was guarding the *Bridal Sweet*? Answers: *don't know*, *don't know* and *no one*.

The first brother jumped up. 'It doesn't matter, Uncle won't rise. It won't want that mutated boy!'

Amber closed her eyes. She had done something foolish and now she was going to have to admit to it. When she was taking Ewan to the Founder she had thought, what harm? If Ewan wanted to join Lough Linger maybe he would go all the way. He had no parents, no one would miss him. A spare Bride might have been useful. 'I brought Ewan to the Founder,' she said. 'He gave Ewan his approval. Uncle won't want Andrew, but will reach out for Ewan.'

'Yes,' said Mr Swift from the podium. 'I was able to explain to Ewan the meaning of the Founder's handshake and his "approval". He's a brave boy. He's using his own soul as bait.'

Villagers jumped to their feet. Betty Bird screamed.

Mr Swift enjoyed his next move. He seized up his cane and pointed down the aisle with it, towards the doors and the lake beyond. 'And he's doing it right now!' he shouted.

Villagers scrambled. Chairs were knocked over in the rush. The doors were thrown open.

'They're out on the boat!' yelled Mr Foster.

The *Bridal Sweet* was on the lake and edging into darkness. Andrew was weighing down the stern, making the bow point high out of the water. Ewan's weight there made no difference. He was facing the village, straining on the oars. Everyone ran to the shore and shouted at them to come back. The boys ignored them and slipped beyond the village lights. Soon no one could see anything but the night.

Somewhere out there, the giant was stirring. Andrew and Ewan would be far from the first fifteen-year-olds to meet Uncle. But it would be a first if they returned.

The villagers peered into the silent darkness for three minutes, four minutes, five. Then a howl rolled from the middle of the lake. The howl was loud, long and mournful. It was not from Uncle. It was coming from Andrew. His cry echoed between the hard hills.

21

Everything had gone according to plan. Mr Swift had the attention of the whole village. Ewan led Andrew to the jetty. It was easy to persuade him to pick up the *Bridal Sweet* and drop it in the water. The old Andrew liked boats, perhaps the monster-boy did too. With Andrew's weight aboard there was only a few centimetres of draught around the stern. Wobble too much and they would surely be flooded. Ewan climbed carefully up to the bow. He had never rowed before but was confident that it was a logical procedure. He fitted the oars into place then reached, dipped and dragged. Sure enough, the vessel moved.

'Hoommmme?' said Andrew.

'No,' said Ewan. 'Not yet.'

Andrew scowled at him. Ewan felt bad. Were Andrew's instincts telling him that his supposed friend was rowing him into danger? Into a deadly fight without his consent? May would never have allowed this.

189

'I am sorry,' he said to the clueless monster-boy. 'I don't know if I am doing the right thing, or the smart thing, or just something selfish.'

It was then that the community centre doors flew open. The villagers poured out and called to them. Ewan dragged more solidly on the oars. The *Bridal Sweet*'s bow was furrowing the lake. There was no other movement on the water.

'But I'll be with you all the way,' Ewan said after a while. 'I think you've a fair chance of winning. You've got a track record for killing monsters. I know you probably wouldn't like the idea but, Andrew, you have always been a champion. It could be you were born to do this. You could be a natural-born monster-killer.'

That was when Andrew howled his heartbreaking howl. Ewan almost dropped the oars. Perhaps Andrew could understand more than anyone realised, more than Andrew himself realised. He looked at Ewan reproachfully as the echo of his cry faded. Right then the villagers were wondering what Andrew's howl meant. Only Ewan had an idea.

'I am sorry,' he said. 'I know you don't want to be a killer. You just want to go home.'

'Hoooommme.'

The *Bridal Sweet* crept the line between surface and sky. Fat drops peeled off the oars as Ewan tugged them from the water. They were approaching the middle of the lake.

Ewan jumped when there was a rapid crackle, like fireworks popping.

It was Andrew cracking his knuckles.

At that moment Uncle was waking, gathering under the hull of the *Bridal Sweet* and gently, lovingly, stroking it.

A sharp minty smell. Ewan could not tell where it came from. 'Do you feel something?' he asked.

Andrew growled.

The water thickened, folding from the oars like cake mix. The boat stopped and Andrew gripped the sides in alarm. It had stopped moving entirely, not the slightest undulation that you would expect from a floating vessel. Ewan let go of the oars. They did not splash in the lake, they bounced against it. He reached over the side and dabbed at the water. The surface had turned to jelly. Fascinated, Ewan ran his hand along it. Stringy bits came away as the water's waxy skin broke up and gelled again. Dots of blue light began to twinkle deep below. It was like the phosphorescence Ewan had seen in nature documentaries about southern seas. But this was no harmless glowing algae. These lights zipped around, leaving trails. These lights were rising and multiplying.

Ewan heard Andrew's jaw lock into battle-mode. He could smash a big wooden toy but could he handle the real Uncle?

Not a chance, Amber had said.

A few metres away Lough Linger bulged. The mound was full of blue lights. The bulge expanded, slapping against the *Bridal Sweet* and rocking it. Soon it was higher than the boys' heads, quivering like a fat belly but almost silent. It was eyeless. It was mouthless. It smelled like toothpaste.

Uncle is a jellyfish?

But the mound was not sticking out of the lake like something afloat. The blob and the lake were made from the same paste. The water had transformed into a thick goo, separating and resealing itself before their eyes. Waxy dribbles ran down it, like the melt from a candle, but ran up it as well. The gunk seemed to ooze in and out of reason. In and out of logic. Just looking at it made your brain ache.

Things got weirder.

The bulge's peak oozed high into the air, streaks of white fat rolling off it and melding back down onto the lake's shifting skin. The highest part of the growth spat globules of waxy stuff before dividing into a set of wiggling worms. Both Ewan and Andrew flinched from the multi-tipped thing but could not tear their eyes from it. It was like some pale, wriggling life form you might find under a stone. Except this was massive. And getting bigger. There were five worms, each threaded with phosphorescence.

Fingers.

A hand.

The semi-transparent hand then a whole arm surged up. It had four fingers, a thumb, a palm. Then it had a wrist and an elbow. It stretched, like the arm of someone yawning. But it was not a giant's arm reaching out of the water. It was the lake itself that was thickening and stretching into this jelly limb.

The boat slopped in the paste. Andrew was up. His meaty breath overwhelmed the jelly's sour tang. The arm's soft glow reflected in his eyes, blue and yellow mixing to create green. The arm angled over their heads. Ewan had a flashback, for a split second he was a toddler again, helpless and about to be picked up by a gigantic adult, his father perhaps.

Ewan snapped out of it and had a more sensible reaction. Terror.

'Andrew!'

Tenderly, the thumb pressed on Ewan's chest, nestling him against the soft fingers. The spongy pressure was not enough to hurt. Ewan was plucked from the *Bridal Sweet* like a flower.

Andrew snarled and sprang. He used his entire body to grab the jelly arm, wrapping his arms and legs around it and clenching every muscle. Uncle's arm flung itself right and left, trying to shake off the monster-boy. Ewan was thrown around like a rag doll. Andrew gritted his teeth and squeezed. He put his whole strength into that squeeze, crossing his arms and legs tighter and tighter. With a muffled belch

193

the arm went peculiar. Andrew had forced the arm's waxy innards up into the hand. The arm was squeezed skinny and the hand bloated, Ewan gasped as Uncle's fingers ballooned against him. Andrew squeezed tighter, compressing the arm to a stem. Now Ewan could not breathe. The hand got fatter and fatter, losing all detail as it swelled.

SLRUUPE! A fingertip burst and its innards gushed out.

Ewan felt huge relief. Four more explosions followed. Each finger had reached capacity and their tips split open. Five fountains of watery flesh gushed into the air. Lots splashed back down on Ewan, covering him in strings of jelly. But at least he could breathe.

Then he was falling.

The arm was sucked back into the rubbery lake, turning itself inside out as it retracted. Ewan bounced high against the surface. When he came back down the second time it was with a splash. Lough Linger was water again. The phosphorescence flickered out. The *Bridal Sweet* was floating normally only a few metres away.

'Good work,' said Ewan as Andrew grabbed him by the collar and hoisted him aboard. 'But I don't think you killed it.'

They had seen what happened. The limb had formed itself from the water. What *was* this lake?

People drank from it, fish lived in it. Could it also be a monster? Was Uncle the lake itself? One thing was certain: 'It's bigger than we thought,' said Ewan.

The monster-boy's body still throbbed with high alert, a growl rattling about inside him. Andrew's instincts said the creature was not done with them yet. Andrew's instincts were never wrong. Ewan heard a high pitch running through the growl that reminded him of a cornered animal. He realised that Andrew was frightened.

They listened, two boys bobbing up and down in a small boat, waiting for a monster. They could hear voices carrying faintly from the village, but that only heightened the sense of isolation and exposure. Andrew's brain tried to lock onto floating images, memories he could not quite grasp. A grey house he once knew. A man and a woman and two small boys who looked like him. Cabbages in shopping bags. The smell of polish. What were these things? Why did they seem so desperately important right now?

Phosphorescent dots came alive again in the deep. They moved faster this time, smearing streaks of light as they dashed to shore. Soon there was a vast splatter of lights down there, like a galaxy caught in glue. The whole lake was aglow. Ewan could see the silhouettes of fish swimming about. Cries of astonishment came from the villagers. This was obviously something they had never witnessed before.

The lights were beautiful.

The lights were terrifying.

'I think we've hurt Uncle,' said Ewan.

They had. Uncle had been attacked. It had been rejected. Uncle could not stand rejection. It had something that might be described as *feelings*. They were hurt. Now it would do something that might be described as *screaming*. Uncle was going to be revealed for the first time in centuries.

22

The *Bridal Sweet* rose a few centimetres, flopped to one side and lay still. The lake had pulled taut under its hull. Every atom of the surface was gelling to its neighbours in abnormal ways. Lough Linger was sprung like a huge trampoline. Right now Andrew and Ewan could have walked back to shore.

Or run.

Without warning Lough Linger heaved. Put a paper boat on a tablecloth and shake out the cloth from one end, it would be an impression of how the *Bridal Sweet* was bounced over the surface. The boys clung on as the boat hopped then rocked to a stop. Gripping the sides of the *Bridal Sweet*, Andrew cracked two planks.

The middle of the lake bulged again in fits and starts. The swelling was already the height of a house. Drips ran up and down its sides. Each spasm flicked the boat further back towards the village. The fleshy hillock glowed blue and pulsed angrily. Fatty ridges were forming, running from the peak, denser and darker than the rest of the creature. The ridges in turn gave birth to rows of quivering blossoms. Each dripped wax and was two metres long, surging from the mother-lode. They slapped noisily, the consistency of rubber. Many sproutings had five growths at their ends but they spat and shivered and failed to look like fingers. Some sprouting tops looked more like melted people, a squished head and two arms and legs kicking and twisting.

The *Bridal Sweet* was lifted as the lake became a dome. A hill of quivering jelly, glowing, and still growing. The boat slid down its side, fast then faster, cutting a trench through Uncle's flesh. Andrew and Ewan hung on. Then the inevitable happened, the *Bridal Sweet* struck one of Uncle's ridges and flipped. Boys and boat went separate ways, the *Bridal Sweet* spinning into the night. The boys hit Uncle's side and were flung down two different furrows. There was nothing to grip. Nothing to grab. The ground, lit blue by Uncle, was racing towards them. Ewan caught sight of the *Bridal Sweet* crashing down first. Its bow crunched against stone and it fanned apart, planks falling in a circle. Seconds later Ewan landed on his back. The hardness under his hand was flat and familiar. He was on the jetty.

He saw the villagers. They were staring, not at him or Andrew but up. Way up. The villagers used to stand here to look across the lake but now, instead, they were looking up at a quivering hill. Uncle was huge and horrendous, so big and round that its peak was out of sight. Along its ridges fat sproutings, hundreds of them, smacked against each other loud and furious. Their rippling was hypnotic. No one could put accurate words on the smell of its fumes but neither would anyone forget it. The creature assaulted every sense, its mass seemed to bend reality. It was like a hallucination, a glitch in your vision. But there it was, real, massive and utterly in their faces. The citizens of Lough Linger were particularly sheltered and sensitive but any human mind would have been pushed to sanity's edge just by looking upon it. Yet no one shut their eyes to protect themselves. They were mesmerised.

Every upturned face was bathed in blue light. The whole valley was. In the plantations, birds were singing and mammals were scurrying to their burrows; it was so bright they thought dawn had come early. Along the hilltops deer stood frozen by the sight of the life form. Its glow was reflected in their wide eyes.

Uncle's insides were thickening now too. Fish could be seen through its dripping skin, swimming slowly through dense water. More dense by the second.

Ewan crawled away before the creature made another grab for him.

Villagers began to shriek. They had just seen their

own history inside Uncle's body – it was written in corpses. The Brides of the Lake were suspended throughout its pasty innards. Many were silhouetted shapes hanging limp in the glow. Other bodies were close enough for their faces to be seen. The villagers saw Brides that no one remembered, Brides given to the lake centuries ago, their clothes quaint and frilly. But they also saw faces they knew, their own aunts or uncles kept permanently at the young age the creature had claimed them. Mr Swift broke his eyes away, afraid he might see Molly. He staggered off, crying and cursing. Number three of the brothers Earlly was visible, fifteen forever. The living brothers looked at each other's old faces then back at their dead third. It was like looking back in time. The Fosters wailed when they recognised their firstborn child hung in the paste. And what were those horrible attachments? They looked like fleshy tubes inserted into his ears. Uncle's arteries wound between all the Brides, hooking them up to its monstrous system. Every Bride had a few worming into their ears, nostrils or mouth. They were forever part of Uncle now.

Villagers screamed when a girl's eyes flicked open.

'They're alive in there!' yelled Mrs Melody.

The girl's eyes had definitely opened but she gave no other sign of life. Maybe she could see them. Maybe she had been dead for three hundred years.

'I swear he moved his hand!' shouted Farmer Able, pointing to a boy hung cruelly upside down.

'They're trying to shout to us!' cried Thomas Farr.

Maybe they were. It was difficult to tell. Maybe Uncle's rapid quivering was sending vibrations through its body and making the Brides seem to move. But some did appear to be mouthing words or screaming. Their eyes gleamed with paralysed insanity.

CRUNCH.

Granite shattered. Uncle's expanding body pushed at the shore, making it crack and rupture. The villagers ran back as the jetty folded over. A slab of shore was flipped, tossing over the Honeyfords' cottage. Ripped electricity cables and water mains whirred in the air. The destruction brought everyone to their senses. If the creature got much bigger the village would be crushed under its bulk.

'Uncle is crying for help,' Amber Feather shouted as she marched through the crowd. 'We've got to make it happy again. We know what it needs, don't we? A soul to soothe it.'

Villagers turned to look at Ewan. Normally they were a healthy-looking lot, fresh and rosy. But now Uncle's blue glow made them appear ghoulish and full of shadows.

'Now you see what Uncle's really like,' Ewan shouted desperately to everyone. 'You can't want it anymore!'

'Don't you get it?' Amber shouted as she urged everyone towards Ewan. 'Our love for Uncle is stronger than anything.'

The brothers Earlly had gotten over the sight of their third brother and were coming for Ewan.

'Look! It's dying!' Ewan was really screaming now. 'Let it die!'

Had any villagers looked they would have seen that indeed the fish were pumping with all their might just to move centimetres. The monster's body was seizing up. Grey patches were appearing on its skin. The sproutings were ripping themselves up and squirting fat. Uncle needed to feel love all the time. One hurtful blow was enough for it to bloat up and die.

Amber, Mr Merriman, Mr Foster, Betty Bird – all had only yesterday been tripping over themselves to make Ewan cups of tea. Now Ewan's feet hardly touched the ground as they dragged him to the monster.

Uncle was hurting and needed a fresh Bride. As soon as Ewan was close, a reaction came over the creature. The whole hill-sized mass of jelly lurched for him. Great chunks of shoreline were pounded down. Two cottages were sucked under its rolling flab. Each sprouting surged in Ewan's direction, like a thousand tongues longing for him. Four fingers and a thumb took shape.

'Let it die!' Ewan was shouting as he struggled.

More patches of Uncle's body were greying and cracking. Flakes of dead skin, the size of blankets, were peeling off and falling to the ground. Ewan was right. Uncle was dying.

But it was still fluid enough to send forth an arm. The arm was three metres long, then five. Uncle's hand was coming for Ewan.

'Hold him still,' Amber ordered. Seven or eight citizens held Ewan stretched out and up in the air.

Ewan in Trouble = Bad.

With a wallop Andrew dropped from somewhere, heaven perhaps. He landed behind the villagers, crouched, bristling and ready to rip the head off anyone. Every hair on his skull was charged and standing straight. His eyes burned like headlamps.

The first of the brothers Earlly leaped on Andrew's back, attempting a stranglehold on his throat. Andrew just shook his shoulders and his attacker was thrown off. The second brother seized his upper arm. Andrew looked at him, grunted and flexed his bicep. The man fell away screaming, both thumbs broken.

The other villagers dropped Ewan when they saw Andrew coming. It did not matter anyway. Something else had happened.

Brigit had stepped between Ewan and Uncle's hand.

The hand lurched for her, dead shredded skin falling from it. Brigit held her arms out in welcome, inviting Uncle to make one last stretch. She knew Uncle could do it. She knew this was meant to be. Everyone watched with their breaths held. Everyone except Ewan.

'NOOO,' he howled, scrambling to save her.

Too late. Brigit's eyes were full of wonder as the hand wrapped around her. She dropped her arms against Uncle's flesh and was pleased by the way they sank in. Her head was flung back as the hand retracted. A splash and a puff of tangy scent and she was under Uncle's skin.

'No, no,' Ewan moaned. He fell to his knees. He was supposed to be saving *her*, keeping her alive. Instead, Brigit had saved his life.

Brigit ascended, still visible to the village. Around her, Uncle's body became softer again. Dead patches flowed once more. Fish were freed to swim on normally. Brigit's hair waved and her body shimmered, dusted with phosphorescence. Right then the monster was flowing into her, suffocating her with its flesh and something else it had, something like love. Uncle oozed with emotion as it swamped the new Bride. The villagers watched her take a place among the sacrificed. Already new arteries were snaking towards her. The monster's pulsing lights slowed to a contented throb. Its sproutings hung down and relaxed. It was quiet as a sleeping child now. Uncle was happy.

After Andrew's attack it had taken Uncle ten minutes

to congeal and bulge to hill-size. But it needed only seconds to return to liquid. The sproutings retracted and its body melted back down, drawing the Brides down with it. With a few metres to go Uncle was already water. It collapsed. The middle of the lake fell beyond flat, becoming concave. Walls of water shot up against the shore and splashed down again. The blue glow shrank then went out. Soon starlight was reflecting on dark calm water. It was Lough Linger again.

23

May approached the campfire. It was being kept well fuelled to stay burning under the rain. Her dad was sitting beneath the canopy of his tent. May stepped into the firelight. He stared, not daring to believe.

'Never thought you'd come looking for me,' he said.

'What were ye waiting for then?' she asked.

'I was going to try talking to you again in a couple of days,' he said.

'And if I'd chased ye again?'

'I'd have waited some more.'

He poured hot water from the blackened kettle on the fire and made her coffee. May warmed her hands against the tin cup but stayed out in the rain.

'Did you see that quare blue light in the sky earlier?' her dad asked.

May shook her head.

'I think it was coming out of that valley you're staying in,' he said.

'Ye wouldn't know what that crowd would be at,' said May.

She sipped her coffee and edged around the fire, coming almost under the canopy.

'I'd like you to come home with me,' said her dad.

'Home's a place I haven't found yet,' she said.

That wounded him, but he knew it was fair. 'Ach, well,' he said, 'in the meantime you'll need somewhere to stay.'

May looked over her shoulder. 'I might look for a good strong ledge,' she said.

They gazed into the fire a while. May's dad counted his blessings. At least she was talking to him. At least she had come under the canopy.

May glanced around his set-up. There was about a month's supply of sardines and Pot Noodles. The tent was the heavy canvas type, patched up here and there. Inside the flap was a stack of books. They all had titles like *Positive Thinking* and *Daily Wisdom*. He seemed to be hooked on self-help books. There were worse things to be hooked on.

'May,' he said, 'let me look after you.'

'Grew up kinda wild, didn't I?' said May. 'Hard to handle, with me ability and all?'

'I'm proud of you,' he said.

They both let his statement sit, as if it was something he often said. As if it was not the first time he had ever said those words to May in her entire life.

'I might have to try being ordinary,' said May with a sniffle. 'But I hate the thought of it. I might chicken out. Somewhere along the way I've come to hate the idea of being ordinary more than anything.'

May looked around, sensing so much. Each ditch was a kingdom, alive with the intrigue of hedgehogs. A badger was sniffing his way home, looking forward to his cub's contact. The thick grasses contained nests and told her a dozen feathered love stories. Slugs were concentrated on the ground, slow but unstoppable. Few people appreciated the steely determination of slugs. But May did. She understood this and much, much more. This was her world.

'What's it like, being ordinary?' she asked her dad.

He was raising his cup to his mouth but paused and brought it down again. 'I didn't think I was the authority on it,' he said, but the sight of his daughter's faint smile brought him such joy he was prepared to accept anything. He stretched out, as if about to recount a long tale of ordinariness. But all he said was, 'It means having to *try*. Try every day.'

'Sounds awful boring,' said May.

'It can be,' he admitted and he glanced towards his books. Then he seemed annoyed with himself for not being positive or cheerful enough. He reacted quickly to make up for it, too quickly. He leaned over and patted her on the back, too hard. 'We're a good team, aren't we?' he said.

May did not say anything.

'And don't worry about being ordinary,' he said. 'Everything will be grand. Come home with me. We'll look out for each other. We've always been a good team, haven't we? May?'

May looked at him with a sad smile.

Next morning May helped her dad pack his tent. They parted, for a while anyway. May headed back through the rain to Lough Linger. She followed the track between two of the valley's hills. When she stepped beyond the rain's edge she paused to take in the view. The lake was more tranquil than ever. Mist rose from the slinky surface, as if the water were light as air. Tomatoes, potatoes and rows of cabbages were absorbing sunlight, you could almost hear them grow. But where were the workers? They would normally be in the fields by now, chatting and singing while they pruned, picked or shovelled. But there was no sign of anyone. Then May saw the damage. Fences had fallen and sheep were wandering loose. The jetty was crumpled. At least two cottages were crushed, nothing left of them but broken blocks and flattened thatch. May noticed another change. She spent a while studying the shore before she could be certain of it. Rocks that had poked up into the air before were now underwater. The lake had gotten bigger.

May heard the squeal of an overworked bicycle. She waited to see who was approaching. Tim laboured up the track out of the valley and into view, riding a BMX. He had a pack on his back and was already sweaty from the climb. His red hair and red face were both redder than usual. When he saw May he skidded to a stop.

'Where are ye goin'?' asked May.

'Away,' he said. He looked embarrassed, a kid caught with his hand in the biscuit box.

'Away?'

'We saw Uncle last night,' said Tim, gesturing towards the crushed jetty, 'and . . . and I don't want to be a Bride of the Lake anymore. I don't want to be sacrificed to that *thing*.'

'So there is a monster,' said May.

Tim gulped. 'Monster,' he said, thinking about May's word. 'Yes,' he decided. 'That's what Uncle is. That's what Uncle has been all along. So I'm leaving.'

'Ye'll take your chances in the big bad world?' asked May.

'Is it really as bad as they say?' Tim asked in a small voice.

From where they were standing, May and Tim could see both in and out of the valley. One way led to the sun-kissed Lough Linger. The other disappeared under banks of rain. Beyond the rain were mean towns, polluted cities, warring nations and billions of people obsessing over billions of different things.

'I'll not lie to ye,' said May. 'It's a mess.'

'I'm going to take my chances,' said Tim.

Tim checked his tyres and took off his pack to adjust the contents. May saw a milk bottle and some biscuits in there. At no point did Tim look back towards Lough Linger. May saw resolve in him. The hint of a backbone. Maybe the boy would be all right.

'Goodbye, May.'

'Mind yourself.'

Tim jumped on the pedals and was off. Gone, into the rain. Off into the world with nothing on his side but a pint of milk and three packets of Bourbon Creams.

Giving the village a wide berth, May went to the lakeshore. She climbed up onto the boulder she and Ewan often sat on. From there she communed with the swans resting on the lake, asking them to leave for a while. They launched in a white storm and were soon vanishing over the hills. May sighed at their splendour.

'Should've seen what happened last night,' said a voice and May spun around. Theodora was hovering by her shoulder. She was seated in the middle of a school bench, stolen from Mr Swift's classroom. She was full of gossip and eager to share. 'Turns out Uncle isn't *in* the lake,' said Theodora. 'Uncle *is* the lake. It's like, *living water*. And everyone's being drinking it!' She laughed.

May looked from Theodora to the lake and back again. 'Are Andrew and Ewan all right?' she asked.

'They're grand,' she said. 'Everyone is. Apart from Brigit.'

May looked again over Lough Linger. 'The water *itself* is a monster?' she said.

'Crazy, huh?'

'But a monster needs a mind of some sort,' said May. 'I didn't feel one, even when ye dropped me in it.'

That humiliated Theodora. She lost height. 'Yeah, sorry about that,' she said, as she floated up again. 'Maybe it keeps its brain tucked away somewhere. Uncle only revealed itself at all because it was upset. It went all freaky and bloated, like it was made from the nasty fat chunks in bacon. Someone attacked it. Guess who?'

May raised her eyebrows.

'Ewan brought Andrew out to scrap with Uncle.'

'Ewan did *what*!' said May. 'He'd no right!'

Theodora had not expected May to be angry, although she now realised she should have done. May was always worrying about the monster-boy. Theodora rocked to and fro in the air, thinking about it. 'Don't go too mad at Ewan,' she advised. 'Boys will be boys. Often dumb, but magnificent at the same time.'

May fumed a while. Theodora waited, letting her

get over it. She lay sideways on the bench, resting her head on one hand. 'Ewan put his life on the line too,' she said. 'He used his own soul to lure the monster up. If Andrew had failed to hurt it, Ewan would have been dinner.'

'Must have a good soul, that Ewan,' said May, with a touch of bitterness. 'Your monster had the chance to take my life but I guess it didn't want me.'

'Had a chance to take mine as well,' said Theodora, remembering the night she had waited out on the lake. 'It didn't want me, either.'

That did not make May feel any better.

'I see you chased off the swans,' said Theodora. 'Was that in case I use them to beat someone up when I have your power?'

Theodora knew she had won but she did not gloat. She liked May. Had things been different they could have been friends. Having a friend might be nice. Theodora would have preferred to take only a share of the ability. Even just borrowing it for a few hours would be fine. A few hours was all she needed. But that was not how it worked. The ability would be separated from May and become Theodora's completely. Then it would be part of Theodora until she died.

'So . . . how's this done?' asked May.

Theodora did not reply. Instead she floated over so their faces were close. May gulped and closed her eyes. Then, much to her surprise, Theodora kissed her.

24

No amount of tea and scones could calm the people. They could not even face a cup of tea. Trusty pots no longer looked the same. Steam curled maliciously from their spouts. People looked at each other. 'Cup of tea?' they said, but without heart.

The villagers tried to shake the memory of the gigantic blob and the tortured bodies within it. But it was impossible. Often they had wondered if Uncle was a kind of man or woman, hours they had spent discussing it. What fools they had been, it was neither. Uncle, they realised, was a monster and the monster was the lake. When they drank from Lough Linger they were, in fact, taking a transfusion direct from the creature. The old people knew they were bound tightest with Uncle. It was Uncle in their bodies that kept them alive. They were hardly more distinct from the monster than the rubbery sproutings that dangled from its body. They were just a part of its beastly system. The monster could not walk or fly.

How did it find the souls it needed? It grew them within reach. Just like the villagers tended sheep and cabbages, the monster tended them. It farmed them for their children.

Bonding with a gigantic, ancient, faceless, child-eating blob – the people of Lough Linger did not approve of things like that.

'Lesser-Spotted Blossoms!' Mrs Hume said suddenly, her eyes wide and anxious in her glasses. 'They aren't plants at all! The sproutings were part of the beast. They pushed up through the ground from the bottom of the lake. Growing straight from that monster's body! And we thought they were flowers and loved them! We all gathered and—'

Mrs Hume stopped herself with a shudder. She looked around her tabletop. Everything seemed tainted: the tea cosy, the milk jug, the pine table itself. There was nothing on which her eyes could comfortably rest. Even the backs of her own hands were sickening to her. 'Uncle owns us, doesn't it?' she said.

Mr Hume was seated at the other end of the table but had not heard her. He was stroking his white beard and staring vacantly into space.

Villagers gathered in the community centre, under the stained glass window. A few panels had fallen out. Last night's ructions had shaken the building. The foundations had split, making a crack in the floor that ran down the aisle from the doors to the podium. Mr Swift marched along it now, jabbing his cane at everyone. 'The time has come,' he was saying. 'Time to reject the monster.'

'That'll offend it,' warbled Betty Bird.

'That's exactly what will kill it,' said Mr Swift assuredly.

'*That*,' said Amber Feather, standing up at the front, 'is exactly what will kill all of *you*.'

Amber took in the crowd in one long gaze. There were many empty seats today. People were leaving Lough Linger. The Farrs had gone with their new baby. The Fosters had closed up the tea shop and left with their daughters. The man from the *Bugle* had gone. There was no more good news. Mrs Honeyford had finally hiked somewhere other than around the lake. Before dawn she had left the valley with her family. But many had stayed. Amber saw grey hair, liver spots and gnarly hands resting on laps. It was the old who remained.

It was easy to frighten old people.

Frightened people were easy to control.

She could win this argument yet.

Amber spoke. She spoke with strong, positive words but kept the correct level of solemnity. She made eye contact with everyone, one by one, during her speech, walking up and down the aisle. She told them that not just Brigit but many generations of Brides had sacrificed themselves for the valley's endless era of love. To turn their backs on the tradition would be to betray all of them. She conceded a few things. No one could believe that the Brides lived on with Uncle anymore. They died. Their love and their life force went to Uncle. They might even experience some suffering in their final moments. But it was mere seconds. A small price to pay so a whole community could avoid the trouble the rest of the world endured. This was the genius of their arrangement with Uncle. All suffering was compressed into a small spoonful that the Brides of the Lake swallowed on behalf of everyone else.

It was a powerful speech. Villagers mumbled in agreement, getting louder and louder until they were singing together, 'Yes, yes, yes.'

'No!' shouted Miss Boswell, springing to her feet. Everyone stared. Miss Boswell had never shouted in her life. 'We saw them last night,' she said. 'They saw us. The Brides don't even get the relief of dying. They are trapped and suffering forever. They were saying, "Please help us. Please help us."'

Amber gave Miss Boswell a pitiful look. 'We saw no such thing,' she said. 'How much sugar have you been putting in your almond fingers?'

Carrick McCuddy stood up. He was wearing his blood donation medals across the lapel of his best jacket. 'We all got a fierce fright last night, it's true,' he said. 'I thought I saw the Brides moving too. How horrible to think they might be in immortal agony like that. But now I've realised that I was just overexcited at seeing Uncle. They weren't moving at all.'

'Yes,' said Mrs Melody, 'some of their eyelids got flipped open but it was only because Uncle was . . . having a little wobble.'

'Indeed,' said Mr Hume, standing up as Mrs Melody sat down. He stroked his white beard. He was upright as ever but looking closely you might have seen the vacancy in his eyes. 'The Brides go in peace, I'm sure of it. As for Uncle, it's not quite what we thought but nothing's *really* changed, has it? We depend on the creature. The creature depends on us. It's just not as handsome as we thought. And slightly bigger.'

'*Slightly* bigger!' scoffed Mr Swift. 'It's the whole lake! We feed it and it keeps growing. Is that what we want to live for?'

'We do more than just live!' shouted Amber. 'We excel! You're too bitter to get it, aren't you? The simple heart of who we are?' Amber almost sang her next words, a tuneful note coming out of nowhere, 'We love Uncle and Uncle loves us!'

She stopped and looked to the double doors. They were creaking open. Ewan and the monster-boy entered the community centre.

Amber strode down the aisle towards them. 'I thought you'd have run away,' she said. Ewan could

218

see a vicious adversary in her contorted face. Only the villagers' presence was stopping her from lashing out at him. Or perhaps it was Andrew's presence.

The monster-boy detected the Mayor's aggression. He grunted at her.

'Your gorilla keeps you safe,' said Amber, 'but you're no longer wanted here. Leave.'

'We'll be leaving soon enough,' said Ewan.

'Why delay?' hissed Amber. 'You failed to save Brigit. She's with Uncle now.'

That stung Ewan. He wanted to hurt Amber back. 'We're staying to hear you admit that Mr Swift was right all along,' he said. Ewan smiled in a false way, calculated to infuriate Amber. It worked.

Ewan and Andrew sat in the last row. The brothers Earlly glared at them from across the aisle. The second brother had his hands wrapped in bandages, both thumbs stuck up in splints. With the monster-boy to protect him, Ewan enjoyed giving them the thumbs-up.

Amber was speaking again at the front of the hall. 'Mr Swift should leave too,' she said. 'We have all witnessed his trickery and hatred of our tradition. Go. Leave this valley to those prepared to honour their arrangement with Uncle.'

'I will see Uncle die if it is the last thing I do,' said Mr Swift and he allowed himself a grim laugh. 'In fact, it *will* be the last thing I do. But I look forward to it. Yes, it will be for Molly but for Brigit too. For all the

Brides. I cannot count the souls I have seen go to that lake and the amount it has swollen in my lifetime. It makes me sick to think of it.'

Miss Boswell spoke. 'Could that be what Uncle wants, to keep getting bigger?' she asked. 'I'm glad we didn't send the visitors away. It's better that they showed us the real Uncle. Someday, if it's allowed to continue growing, it'll flow out of this valley and flood the mountains. It'll find more villages and they'll probably become like us. Then Uncle will be getting even more Brides.'

'And creating more peace,' insisted Mr Hume, 'and more happiness.'

A hush settled on the community centre as everyone tried to imagine what would happen when Uncle became bigger than the valley. Then wider than the mountains.

'Eventually it would flood the lowlands,' Miss Boswell continued. 'Thousands of people might live by its shore and feed it sacrifices everyday. It would become an inland sea . . .'

'Become a *sea*?' said Mrs Hume, terrified at the idea, whatever her husband's opinion. She removed her glasses and began wiping the lenses methodically. This helped her stay calm.

'Eventually it might smother the whole planet,' said Mr Swift.

'That would take at least fifty thousand years,' said Amber.

Ewan spoke from the back. 'The monster probably doesn't think fifty thousand years is a long time,' he said.

A picture came to Ewan's mind. The far future with Uncle so huge it covered most of the earth's surface, the human race living on islands isolated by thousands of kilometres of crystal-clear water. There would be no Mr Swifts by then, the human race would be given over entirely to taking care of Uncle. Any idea that this was wrong would be long forgotten. In fifty thousand years of drinking from Uncle, humans would probably be three metres tall, graceful, beautiful and live hundreds of years. Singing joyfully, they would dance to the shore with their luckiest children. The children would be singing too, even as they were flung into the sea. They would not stop singing as they sank and Uncle engulfed them, their voices becoming gargles. They would sing and sing, 'We love Uncle and Uncle loves us.'

Ewan felt nauseous. *What will happen if Uncle is not stopped?* The question spun in his mind. The same question divided the villagers. All the citizens were arguing again. Miss Boswell and Mr Swift were in the minority. Most were too afraid of dying. Voices were raised. Mr Hume was saying that a world completely enveloped by Uncle was a wonderful destiny for the human race. Mr Swift yelled that Mr Hume had lost his mind. People were interrupting each other, a thing unheard of in Lough Linger. Farmer Able pounded his fist on the chair in front of him, so distressed it was the only way he could express himself. There was desperation in the air. Andrew snapped his teeth, riled up by the aggression coming off the villagers. The debate became vicious. Some people covered their ears and began to chant, 'We love Uncle and Uncle loves us. We love Uncle and Uncle loves us.'

Ewan was glad to have the monster-boy's protection. Otherwise they might have thrown him in the lake. Perhaps it was time to get out of Lough Linger. But Ewan did not want to leave Uncle alive. Villagers might try to start the tradition again.

Could Andrew and I repeat last night's battle? Ewan wondered. *Myself as lure, Andrew as muscle?*

If they could reject Uncle one more time, hurt it. And if Ewan could keep himself from being sacrificed to soothe the monster then they just might finish it. Last night Uncle had seemed only minutes from death when Brigit stepped in. It was too late to save her but Ewan still wanted to see the end of Uncle.

Unnoticed in the racket May slipped through the doors and sat between her friends. Andrew shook with pleasure when he saw her. She gripped Andrew's arm and Ewan's too. It was good to be all three together again. Andrew, May and Ewan were all of that same instinct, no need to discuss it. They all, including the monster-boy, felt that one raw emotion in the same way.

But May seemed confused, far away. She leaned on their arms, needing support. She looked intently all around her, unblinking. The people, the walls, the roof, everything seemed to fascinate her. 'It's so quiet,' she said.

'With everybody fighting?' said Ewan. 'I bet this is the noisiest meeting they've ever had.'

May registered the debate for the first time. The arguing seemed distant.

Andrew whimpered, he could tell something was wrong. It was like May was in shock. Like she had just staggered from the wreckage of a plane crash.

'Are you okay?' Ewan asked her.

May just looked at him. Some things were too big for words.

25

Theodora's horizons had been ripped wider. The blast had immediately knocked her from the air. She dropped onto the boulder and the bench crashed down beside her. Theodora's mind quaked as new knowledge was pumped in and expanded to fill every chamber. This was a blunt, violent process. She rolled into the tightest ball she could make. Tears burned in her tight-shut eyes. Her brain filled to capacity then more was hammered in. The living world stampeded through her head.

. . . gss . . . bes . . . hewlap . . . cw . . . ghewrss . . . soop . . . cleall . . . bnco . . . saar . . . hig . . . ig . . . ca . . . de . . . rareech . . . cllohosease . . . asmm . . . chaew . . . sancwceim . . . smdmtop . . . carkll . . . sdig . . . bwimabia . . . ch . . . aseere . . . ch . . . baud . . . wbl . . . de . . . caw . . . micm . . . seek . . . reg . . . hodild . . . ipg . . . de . . . dfe . . . dak . . . snibff . . . nar . . . lk . . . cloan . . . laily . . . atrt . . . nsin . . . biendrth . . . fen . . . sedtil . . . mve . . . nreaie . . . mm . . .

She rolled her forehead against the rock, impressing a granite pattern upon it. What was in her head was not pain exactly, but a blaring din. A thousand points of view, all seen at once. A million opinions, all heard in the same moment.

Time.

. . . snibff . . . nar . . . lkaie . . . snibff . . . nar . . . lkaie . . .

To take.

. . . edtil . . . mve . . . edtil . . .

Control.

. . .

Theodora started with her breathing. Regular breathing reduced the intensity. She could not open her eyes but she knew where she was. She could feel the top of the boulder under her cheek. May had run off. She was long gone.

Next Theodora tried digging through the stampede. She dug deep. It took her ten minutes to isolate an experience.

. . . wwsshecarg . . .

For ages she picked at. Prising it apart.

. . . ew wech srags . . .

Then she slotted it back together again.

. . . WeHecwRagss . . .

Nonsense. She tried again.

. . . WeChewGrass . . .

It was coming from close by. Theodora opened her

eyes. A sheep was on the path, loose from its field and looking at her as it worked the grass between its stubby teeth. Theodora discovered that sheep were just as dumb as she had suspected. This one was looking in her direction but hardy saw her really, she was just somewhere for it to point its eyeballs while it chewed.

Theodora sat up. She focused on the sheep. The volume went down on the other animals around.

Come here . . .

Theodora was startled by how effective it was. The dumber the animal, she figured, the easier they were to control. The sheep ambled towards her, stepping off the path and onto rocks where it had no business it to be. No grass was growing on the rocks.

. . . *WeChewGrass?* . . .

Soon, thought Theodora, *first, come here* . . .

The sheep struggled up the round boulder. It slid back, a great ball of wool bouncing against stones. It stood, shook itself and tried again. Its hooves clopped against rock as it kicked up. At the top it looked around, confused as to why it put so much effort into getting there.

With the palm of her hand Theodora lifted the school bench. She swung it under her and floated backwards.

Come here . . .

The sheep obeyed. It wanted nothing more than to go to her.

Theodora floated out over the water.

Come here . . .

The sheep did not stop when the boulder curved down. It did not stop when it was too late to stop anyway. It did not stop until it fell in the lake.

Sheep normally bleat. This was more like squealing, it sounded like a human child. The sheep kicked in terror. Its front hooves scraped at the boulder's underside. The rocks were too round, the sheep had no chance of getting ashore. Its wool became waterlogged. Every moment it was taking on more weight. Theodora watched as it slowly tired. The sheep stopped crying, its panic hardening into a resigned silence. It went under and drowned.

A small bird hit the stained glass window. As the villagers looked up it fell away, leaving a crack in a glass panel. It was only then that everyone, including Andrew, May and Ewan, noticed the chirping. Mr Swift stopped speaking and stared up at the roof. The chanting people uncovered their ears and heard it too. The chirping was getting louder. Birds' feet were scraping the slates. Each joist creaked as more birds landed. There was volley after volley of sharp taps as every slate was pecked at. The villagers would have thought it sounded like hailstones had they known what hailstones sounded like. The entire roof must have been covered in hundreds of birds. Maybe thousands. Then there was the atmospheric pressure of a storm gathering. Every wing began beating. The roof joists creaked again, but in relief this time. The birds took off and flew away.

Villagers glanced back at May. She refused to look up.

'It wasn't her,' Ewan said grimly.

A shadow came over them. Darkness was filling the stained glass window. A storm cloud rolled in low and right at them. It struck the window and shattered it. The dark cloud streamed through the gap, raining glass. It was a cloud of infinite detail: beaks, feathers, claws and thousands of wits. The birds had been gathered from all around the valley. Individually they were sparrows, thrushes, blackbirds or starlings. United, they were a black and brown blur.

Theodora swooped in the window among them. She was standing on a rowboat's broken-off starboard side, riding it like a surfboard.

'Yeaaaaa!'

She whooped with delight.

Villagers dropped to the ground as the birds beat against the air and along the walls. Theodora flew down and cruised the length of the aisle. She stood with feet apart, arms folded, glaring defiantly at the cowering villagers. Her transportation's broken ends scraped along the floor. The crumpled bow was raised forwards displaying the words *Bridal Sweet*. At last, Theodora had a taste of what she wanted. To ride the *Bridal Sweet* towards her destiny while the village looked on. She raised her chin proudly as she travelled the aisle. Her mackintosh and silvery hair streamed behind her. The birds were her bridesmaids. This was her special day.

Then Andrew ruined everything.

He did a footballer's sliding tackle, coming at the girl from the side. His kick sent the remains of the *Bridal Sweet* spinning, bowling twenty chairs over. Theodora fell and her concentration was broken. Birds whooshed back out of the window while others panicked against the roof. Theodora landed on top of the monster-boy. She knelt up on his chest and punched him solidly on the chin.

'Meat-head!' she shouted. 'It took ages to organise that!'

Andrew snarled and seized her throat.

'Don't you want to go home?' choked Theodora.

Andrew let go of her. 'Hoooomme?' he mumbled, disarmed for a moment.

A moment was all Theodora needed. She leaned in. That was when Andrew had his first kiss. He would never forget it.

It was like someone reaching down your throat, rummaging around in your ribs and, one by one, plucking them out. Theodora kept her mouth pressed to his. Andrew's body convulsed, bouncing up and down on the spot. His knuckles beat the ground. Stunned by the sight, villagers clung to each other. Theodora raised her head. Her lips and gums were stained black. Theodora's original power was about *taking things*. Between her teeth now were several black worms that she had taken from Andrew. They were still wriggling, alive with violence and cruelty. Theodora spat them out and crushed them with the heel of her hand. Andrew was gasping for breath, gasping with disbelief. Theodora went in for more.

Who was this? What was this? What was *what* anyway? These were Andrew's first real questions in months. His brain was coming back online. His skin loosened as his frame shrank. Clumps of hair fell out. His teeth normalised. His eyes humanised.

The next time Theodora looked up, her audience had come closer. May and Ewan were watching from among the villagers. She grinned at them all, a worm squirming between her teeth. She bit it in half to impress everyone. It was impressive, in a way.

Andrew coughed and spluttered. He took massive gulps of air, as if he had been holding his breath for six months. He was small inside his clothes now. His ankles and wrists looked comical disappearing into folds of cloth. Theodora got up and stood over him, examining the results of her treatment. May and Ewan knelt by his side. He opened his eyes.

'Andrew?' said May.

'Maaaaay,' he whispered.

'One arm is still mutated,' said Theodora. 'But the boy's cleared of those critters.'

Andrew leaned up and looked around. His shoulders were crooked. Sure enough, one arm was still bigger than the other. Andrew looked at the big arm, his eyes now expressive and understanding. 'I'll never be beat at arm-wrestling,' he said.

All the villagers gasped together.

May flopped on the floor.

'Andrew! Listen,' said Ewan. They could celebrate later. Now Ewan wanted to get Andrew up to speed. 'You're in a valley with a village and a lake that's actually a monster. I brought you out to fight it but it's so huge there wasn't much you could do.'

'Yeah, I know,' said Andrew. 'I was there.'

May recovered and was soon hugging him tight. Theodora backed off and pushed her way through the silent villagers. They stepped aside, disturbed by the hatred steaming off her. They could all remember Theodora as a sweet little girl. Now look at her. She was kicking around the furniture, searching for something.

Amber Feather pushed open the double doors. Birds had scratched her face and she wanted to wash the wounds in the lake. Other villagers trailed after her.

Theodora found a broom. It would have to do. Side-saddle, she settled on its handle and aimed for the exit. Before she could move Ewan grabbed the brush end and held her back. 'I think you've made your point,' he said. 'You should leave these people alone now.'

'I'm only getting started,' she laughed. 'Don't you think you're the one who should be running, Mister Chosen Soul?'

Theodora accelerated out of his grip and away. She swept over the villagers' heads and off across the lake.

Ewan saw the brothers Earlly waiting by the doors. Both were making mean grins at him. The first brother gave him the thumbs-up. Andrew was getting to his feet, helped up by May. He was his normal self again. Just another fifteen-year-old boy. Ewan was suddenly worried. Half the village hated them and they were defenceless. Andrew was just Andrew, no longer the monster-boy. May was just May, no longer armed with a powerful ability. Ewan was just Ewan, not special. They were three ordinary teenagers.

Shrieks came from the lakeshore. Villagers ran to see the cause. They discovered what Theodora had been doing while they argued in the community centre. At first the white lumps on the lake looked like chunks of ice, a whole arctic flow of them. But they were not ice. They were drowned sheep. Theodora had driven the valley's flocks into the water. Two hundred woolly corpses were scattered across the surface of the lake.

26

The citizens of Lough Linger stood on the shore and howled over the mass murder. They screamed and cried and pulled at their own hair. Andrew, May and Ewan took the opportunity to escape. They ran along the side of the community centre and up through the village. They hid around the back of Mr Merriman's shed. Here the cries from the lakeside were a low murmur. Mr Merriman's garden was as bountiful as ever, all the gardens and farms were. But the valley felt broken and desperate. The sun shone but the stillness was chilling.

May peeked around the corner to see if they were being chased. They were not. Not yet anyway.

'We'll get ye away from here,' May said to Ewan. 'Them ones are goin' nuts. They might get notions of giving ye to the lake.'

Andrew tightened his belt, making a new hole to fit his shrunken waist. He rubbed his scalp. His hair had fallen out but would grow back in time. The girl in the mackintosh had healed him. He was grateful to her. Then he remembered the sheep. They could see Theodora, a dark figure circling above the lake. She was shrieking and laughing, enjoying the villagers' distress. Andrew had never imagined anything so twisted. Did the villagers deserve Theodora? Maybe, but the sheep did not.

'How was she able to do that?' asked Andrew.

Nobody said anything. Then Ewan came out with it, 'May traded her power with her so she'd cure you.'

Andrew's hands fell. He slumped against the shed. 'Whaaa?' was all he could say.

'It's done now,' said May, peeking around the corner again so the boys could not see her face. 'No good crying about it.'

'But, May . . . what will you do?' asked Andrew.

'Be ordinary,' she said.

'You could never be ordinary,' he said.

'Whatever I am, I am it now and always will be,' said May. 'Before it was easy, I never had to think about stuff. Just being *me* was plenty. But now I'll have to think about what I'll *do* with me. An ordinary girl has to think hardest of all.'

'Ordinary boys too,' said Ewan. 'That's why I am not leaving Lough Linger. Not yet.'

'Ye what?'

'We can't just leave Uncle alive and people ready to restart the sacrifices,' said Ewan. 'There's a man outside the village. They call him the Founder. He knows about Uncle. We should go and speak to him.'

'Clear out of here is what we should do,' said May. 'Tim's gone. I saw him go. You're the only one in danger from Uncle now.'

'As long as Uncle lives, people will be in danger. You saw how frightened the villagers are. They'll start the tradition again. The Mayor will organise it. People will keep getting sacrificed and Uncle will keep getting bigger. And bigger. And bigger. It might never end. Unless we end it today.'

'But what can we do?' asked Andrew. 'I couldn't hurt that creature now. We're all just ordinary, remember?'

'When you fought Uncle,' said Ewan, 'you didn't really injure it. I think it was the pain of rejection it couldn't stand. We should go and tell the Founder that we reject Uncle. I've met the Founder. He claims to be able to talk to the lake. Perhaps he can tell Uncle that it's rejected.'

'*Perhaps*,' said May.

'We have to try something,' said Ewan. 'But if you don't want to help, I'll go alone.'

May and Andrew looked at each other. They knew Ewan meant it. So they knew they were going with him.

They did not meet any villagers on their way around the lake. Rock slabs had been flipped across the path during Uncle's tantrum the night before. They climbed over them and on to the Founder's house. At the door Ewan raised his hand to knock but May snorted at that idea and pushed on in. Andrew shrugged at Ewan and went in after her. Ewan knew the sight inside would stop them in their tracks and he was right. Cold disgust gripped them as soon as their eyes adjusted to the dark chamber. The blankets of mould, the carpet of fungus and the wall-clinging mushrooms keeping a fog of spores in the air. As ever, the Founder was in bed. He was reading *Oliver Twist*. He looked grumpily at them, annoyed at being interrupted, and did not put down the book. He regarded them with his wet eyes. His breathing was like a whirlpool washing up and down.

'We've got a message for Uncle,' said Ewan.

Once, slowly, the Founder blinked. He opened his toothless mouth. 'Uncle loves you,' he said. 'That's all that needs to be known.'

'I do not love Uncle,' said Ewan. 'I hate it.'

Ewan's words caused the Founder to kick. The book fell from his hands, his body arched under the blankets and his eyes rolled back in his head. In fright May and Andrew grabbed Ewan's arms but Ewan pressed on. 'No one loves Uncle anymore!' he yelled. 'Tell Uncle that!'

The Founder's spasm passed. Slowly he sank back into normal position. His deep breathing began again. He picked up his book and gave the teenagers one last glance. 'You've said your piece,' he said. 'Leave me now. I'm trying to read.'

He opened *Oliver Twist* and read as if there was no one else in the room.

Ewan had been hoping for something more definite. The Founder just seemed to find them rude and boring.

'So . . . you'll give Uncle the message?' asked Ewan. 'Tell it that it's been rejected?'

The Founder exhaled, irritated that the teenagers were still in his chamber. 'No,' he said.

'You have to,' said Ewan.

'Why?'

'Because it's the truth.'

'Ah,' said the Founder, looking at Ewan from over the top of his book. 'We discussed the value of honesty before, didn't we? But are you ready for the truth, I wonder? Let me tell you about my selection process, how I chose the Brides. Uncle wants love and it wants freshness, you might call it youth. All three of you have those things. But there's one more essential requirement if Uncle is to want you. The one thing I detected when I touched your hand, Ewan. But you may be disappointed to learn that it's nothing to do with your soul. Uncle has no interest in souls. The last requirement is that you have the correct blood type.' The Founder indicated May and Andrew. 'They both have the wrong type. Incompatible. Uncle could not absorb them. But you, Ewan, you're a perfect match.'

The Founder was repulsive but May could not help but laugh. She laughed out loud. 'So it's nothing to do with souls at all?' she said.

The Founder agreed it was funny. 'I do not dabble in spiritual matters,' he said with a wet smile.

Ewan let this new information sink in. Theodora was rejected just because she happened to have the wrong blood type running in her veins. Brigit just happened to have the right type. As did Ewan. He was not so amused as May. 'So your approval has been random all along?' he said.

'Not random to me, a compatible blood type is vital,' said the Founder. 'But my people like rituals and ceremonies. Letting them talk about souls helped give the tradition more meaning to them. I let them believe it. I will continue to do so and they will keep bringing me Brides.'

'There's no one left here except scared pensioners,' said Ewan. 'All the kids you approved of, they've all gone. Tell Uncle it's finished.'

The Founder watched Ewan for a while. He liked the boy's life force. He remembered the sweet compatibility he felt when he touched his hand. 'If you feel so strongly about it, he said slowly, 'why don't you tell Uncle yourself?'

Ewan stopped and glanced at his friends. 'Can you arrange that?' he asked the Founder, trying not to sound frightened. 'Can we speak directly to Uncle?'

The Founder closed his book and placed it on his lap. He looked at his visitors, his eyes gleaming. 'You are speaking directly to Uncle,' he said.

There were a few seconds of silence before Andrew blurted, '*You're* the monster?'

'Monster, Uncle, Founder,' he said, 'these are all names I have been given. Once I had a clan living by my shore that called me "The Eye of the World". What do I care what humans call me? I'm unique. I require no name.'

'But you came from outside,' said Ewan, backing off with his friends. 'You're the man who found this valley.'

'No, I'm not,' said the figure in the bed. 'That man found a pool and he drank from it. That pool was me. I claimed his body and used it as my model. But I'm not a person at all. What you are looking at is one of my sproutings. I keep it here in human form to talk to my people and make sure they keep supplying Brides. It's also where I do my thinking. This sprouting is where I keep my brain.'

The three teenagers were backed up against the wall.

The figure in the bed said, 'Even if I don't get a fresh Bride I will not be *finished*. My stomach will turn to stone but my mind will just sink back underground. It would not be the first time I've been rejected. I'll resurface eventually and look for love. And if I'm rejected again, I'll try another day. I am rooted deep down. I cannot die. I've all the time in the world.'

That was when the door flew open. Theodora crashed in on her latest transportation, the broom from the community centre. The others ducked away as she spun in the air and landed at the foot of the bed. The figure under the blankets recognised her.

'*You.*'

'Me,' agreed Theodora. She sniffed the sordid dead air with the helpless man wallowing in it. When Theodora was brought here before for an audience with the Founder, this chamber had seemed darkly splendid. Now Theodora saw it for something different, a rotten hole with a sicko at its centre. 'You ruined my life,' she said. 'Ruined it and at the same time forced me to live it.'

'You wanted to believe that souls could be graded according to quality,' said the figure in the bed, 'with yours at the top. But now look at you – vindictive, cruel.'

Theodora shook her silvery hair. 'I'm like this because of you!' she screamed.

'No,' said the figure. 'You decided how to live and you chose badly. Every morning you wake up and choose badly again. This morning you did it for the thousandth time. I have a stomach full of sheep that proves it.'

'You've a *what*?' said Theodora.

'Get away!' Andrew warned her. 'That's not a person. It's just part of Uncle.'

Theodora looked at the feeble man in the bed. Her new ability did not work on people but she tried it on him anyway.

It was like falling to the centre of the earth.

OOOoooOOOOOoooOOooOOOOOooooOOOOOO
OOOOOoooooooOOOOOooooOOOOOOOOOOoooooooo
oOOOOOoooOOooOOOOOooooOOOOOOOOOOOOOo
oooooOOOOOooooOOOOOOOOOOooooOOOOOoooo
OOOOOOOOOOOOOoooooooOOOOOooooOOOOOOO
OOoooooOOOOOoooOOooOOOOOooooOOOOOOOO
OOOOoooooooOOOOOooooOOOOOOOOOOoooOOOO
OoooOOooOOOOOoooooOOOOoooooooOOOOOoooooo
oOOOOOooooOOOOOOOOOOooooOOOOOooooOOO
OOOOOOOOOoooooooOOOOOooooOOOOOOOOOO
OOOoooOOooOOOOOooooOOOOOOOOOOOOOooooo
ooOOOOOooooOOOOOOOOOooooOOOOOooooOOO
OOOOOOOOOoooooooOOOOOooooOOOOOOOOOo
oooOOOOOoooOOooOOOOOooooOOOOOOOOOOOO
OooooooooOOOOOooooOOOOOOOOOoooOOOOOOO
OOOOOOoooooooOOOOOooooOOOOOOOOOOoooooO
OOOOooooOOOOOOOOOOOooooooooOOOOOoooo
OOOOOOOOOOoooooOOOOOoooOOooOOOOOoooooO
OOOOOOOOOOOoooooooOOOOOooooOOOOOOOO
OoooOOOOOooooOOooOOOOOooooOOOooooooOO
OOOoooooooOOOOOooooOOOOOOOOOOoooooOOOO
OooooOOOOOOOOOOOOooooooooOOOOOooooOOO
OOOOOOOOOOOoooOOooOOOOOooooOOOOOOOO
OOOOoooooooOOOOOooooOOOOOOOOOOoooooOOO
OOoooooOOOOOOOOOOOOOooooooooOOOOOooooOO
OOOOOOOoooooOOOOoooOOooOOOOOooooOOO
OOOOOOOOOOoooooooOOOOOoOOOoooOOOOOooo
OOooOOOOOooooOOOOOOOOOOOOooooooooOOO

OOooooOOOOOOOOOooooooooOOOOOoooOOooO
OOOOooooOOOOOOOOOOOOOOOooooOOOOOooo
OOooOOOOOooooOOOOOOOOOOOOoooooooOOO
OOooooOOOOOOOOOooooooooOOOOOoooOOooO
OOOOooooOOOOOOOOOOOOOOOooooOOOOOooo
OOooOOOOOooooOOOOOOOOOOOOoooooooOOO
OOooooOOOOOOOOOooooooooOOOOOoooOOooO
OOOOooooOOOOOOOOOOOOOOOooooOOOOOooo
OOooOOOOOooooOOOOOOOOOOOOoooooooOOO
OOooooOOOOOOOOOooooooooOOOOOoooOOooO
OOOOooooOOOOOOOOOOOOOOOooooOOOOOooo
OOooOOOOOooooOOOOOOOOOOOOoooooooOOO
OOooooOOOOOOOOOooooooooOOOOOoooOOooO
OOOOooooOOOOOOOOOOOOOOOooooOOOOOooo
OOooOOOOOooooOOOOOOOOOOOOoooooooOOO
OOooooOOOOOOOOOoooooooooOOOOOoooOOooO
OOOOooooOOOOOOOOOOOOOOOooooOOOOOooo
OOooOOOOOooooOOOOOOOOOOOOoooooooOOO
OOooooOOOOOOOOOooooooooOOOOOoooOOooO
OOOOooooOOOOOOOOOOOOOOOooooOOOOOooo
OOooOOOOOooooOOOOOOOOOOOOoooooooOOO
OOooooOOOOOOOOOooooooooOOOOOoooOOooO
OOOOooooOOOOOOOOOOOOOOOooooOOOOOOo
ooOOOOOOooooOOOOOooooOOOOOOOOOOOO
OOooooOOOOOooooOOooOOOOOooooOOOOOOOOO
OOOooooooooOOOOOoooOOOOOOOOOOoooooooooO
OOOOooooOOooOOOOOooooOOOOOOOOOOOOO
OOooooOOOOOoooOOOOOO

Theodora's jaw dropped. The Founder's mind was a timeless echo of hunger. It was not human. It was not animal. It was monster.

Andrew dashed over, grabbed the Founder's blankets and whipped them off.

Everyone jumped in shock. The Founder's legs were just rubbery trunks, ending not in feet but in stumps that wobbled helplessly. The blankets hanging to the floor had disguised the sprouting reaching up through the floor, up through the bed frame and a hole in the mattress. What they had been calling the Founder was just a human-shaped growth, rooted in the lake. Bubbles were rolling up and down inside its skin. Its waxy flesh filled a tunnel between the lake and the house, linking body to mind. Between them both ran an ancient urge to find love and keep growing. This was Uncle.

For two full seconds the teenagers' eyes actually stopped working. Such horror could not be handled. Their instincts simply chose not to see it, shutting down their visual organs. The man was, in fact, jelly. The jelly was, in fact, monster. An oozing body that had desires. An oozing evil that could calculate the most cunning way to entrap those desires. To keep them close. To have them to love and to hold.

Uncle spoke, 'There's one thing I've learned from reading your literature,' it said. 'Every human has great potential. It's strongest in the young, but so few

244

of you ever reach that potential.' It sighed, a dank breeze straight from the pit of Lough Linger blowing out between its lips. It stroked its copy of *Oliver Twist*, unconcerned that its disguise was gone and its naked horror exposed. Uncle looked again at its visitors. 'But you're still the best thing to have evolved on this planet. I have developed a taste for you. My hunger will never die.'

Theodora recovered from the shock and took off. She bounced off the ceiling. She slammed one foot down and snapped the brush off her transportation. It left a jagged point. 'So eat this!' she screamed, stabbing down with all her might and all her power of flight.

Living goo fountained into the air. The broom handle stood vertical from Uncle's flesh. The sprouting stared at it for a few seconds. Then it stretched out its stumpy arms and legs and it roared. The roar was gathered from Uncle's whole body, from shore to shore. It roared so loud the roof lifted and the teenagers were blown over. It roared so loud its head flipped open. The roaring pit, where the head used to be, got wider then roared out a limb, a stump like a giant thumb. What had been the Founder was morphing into a palm and fingers. Theodora stared at what she had created.

Andrew, May and Ewan had seen enough. They tumbled outside and were instantly aware of being in shadow. The lake had pulled taut and was bloating. It was already above their heads. Even with the sunshine they could see phosphorescence crackling under the skin. Uncle had been hurt and was freaking out again.

'Had enough of this valley yet?' asked Andrew.

They started running.

27

The land between the lakeshore and the Founder's house shook. Earth rose then split open as a waxy tube, a metre wide, ripped itself out. This was the flesh that connected the lake to its human-shaped protuberance. One end joined its expanding stomach, the other disappeared under the house. But not for much longer. All impression of the Founder had disappeared. It was a hand that smashed through the roof and an arm that pulled back, breaking down the house. The Founder's bed and mattress were around the arm like bracelets. They fell to pieces as Uncle reached up and up. It was grabbing for Theodora.

Theodora had shot up through the disintegrating roof. Wreckage fell away and revealed her, clinging to a wooden roof beam. She burst out and up, aimed for escape.

The monster's arm surged after her.

Theodora flew straight up into the air. She was fifty metres up when—

Sluppp . . .

Caught.

Uncle's thumb and two fingers slapped around Theodora's ankles. She was whiplashed into reverse. The wooden beam was in her hands but she could not fly hard enough to break free. There she was held, way above the ground. A strange calm came over Theodora. She took in the wide view. She could see Uncle's massive body at the other end of the arm. The size of a hill, it was shifting in its crater, faintly blue and dripping fat. She could see dense spots suspended inside it, the Brides of the Lake. The shoreline was fracturing under its weight. She could see the village shaking. She could see slates falling from the roof of the Bride's tower, the tower she had always longed to enter. She could see villagers coming this way along the path, led by Amber Feather. They still looked like sheep.

Uncle's thumb pressed between Theodora's shoulders, squeezing her firmly down into its hand. It was not painful. In fact, Theodora felt a rush of comfort. She had not learned what Andrew, May and Ewan had learned. She was not there to hear the truth about why some were approved while others were not. She did not know she had the wrong blood type.

So, held fifty metres above the ground Theodora suddenly dared to hope that Uncle might change its mind. She was still in its hand and the monster was obviously in need of a soothing Bride right now. Given its desperation, might Uncle not accept her soul after all? Might the arm be about to retract and take her inside the body? Might Theodora be hung among the glorious departed? A Bride of the Lake at last? Her soul forgiven and approved? No.

The arm swung back to a deep angle, taking Theodora down to tree level. She felt animal life among the branches but nothing that could help her now.

The arm catapulted up again, hard and fast.

Woooooosh, the hand opened. Theodora flew faster than she had ever done. So fast she became almost unconscious. The plantation passed under her in a blur. Theodora clung to the roof beam, struggling to gain control of her trajectory. Her soul had been rejected again. More, Uncle had thrown her clear out of the valley. She passed between hills. She felt rain and saw bogland coming at her with tremendous speed. She had six seconds to take control of her flight. She spiralled, smelled marsh and wet grass as she skimmed the ground. Fighting for control, she dipped and rolled, her face slapping against the roof beam. The wood almost snapped in the grip of opposing energies, flying and falling. But flying won. Theodora banked steeply, flew high and away. Alive. Theodora had survived but would never return to these hills. She left still believing she was rejected because her soul was inferior. Fate had made her bad and that was that. The truth was merely that Uncle could not absorb her blood type. But Theodora did not know this and she never would.

Andrew, May and Ewan were also leaving Lough Linger. They ran up through the plantation, weaving among rows and calling if any of them went out of sight. It was difficult for Andrew to run straight. Having one extra-big arm threw his balance. May ran so hard her throat burned. There was no time for the wood's silence to disturb her.

They saw flashes of colour and movement through the trees, coming from every direction. Bright slacks, woolly cardigans and sensible boots.

Villagers.

'Ewan, Ewan,' they were calling. 'Uncle needs a Bride.'

The trio stopped. 'We won't let them get you,' said Andrew.

But the villagers were closing in. 'There's only one of you and so many of us,' they were calling. Was it a plea or a threat? Both, probably.

From behind them a deep thud shook the plantation as Uncle expanded out of its basin. It wanted Ewan. It wanted Ewan desperately. Great drools of flesh avalanched down its side as it lunged onto land. Hundreds of sproutings burst forth and surged into the plantation. Its long arm, done chucking Theodora, swung around and arched into the trees, seeking the boy.

The villagers were there to help it. Mr Hopkins grabbed for Ewan from behind a tree. Ewan yelped, weaved away from him but ran into Mrs Bird. She got her claws into him, scraping his neck and drawing blood. 'Please don't resist,' she said. But Ewan was already gone, leaping over Mr Hume's leg as he tried to trip him up.

THUD.

The plantation jumped, every tree launched then slammed back down. Most trees stayed standing because their roots were matted together, forming one huge fibrous web that was wrapped around the hillside. But no forest could withstand Uncle's rolling weight. The plantation was pressed into the ground as the monster advanced. Uncle was coming. Its long arm grabbed and tugged at the land, helping to drag its bulk behind it. In daylight the monster seemed even more impossible. Nature itself would fail and pervert alongside the creature's shifting flesh and endless splatter. Its sour stink rolled ahead.

Ewan dived behind a tree, panting heavily and planning the next move.

'Please don't resist!' Gloria Melody's cry came through the trees.

'It'll be painless,' called Carrick McCuddy.

'Almost painless,' conceded Wilma Wright.

251

THUD.

The plantation hopped.

May screamed when she came face to face with Uncle. But it was not the real Uncle, who had no face. It was the mosaic around the Bride's tower, already looking like a piece of archaeology. The forgotten god of a simpler time. Andrew arrived next to her.

'In!' Ewan yelled as he ran by.

Inside the compound wall, goats were dashing about in panic. Andrew, May and Ewan dragged the swing set over the lawn and wedged it against the door.

'Uncle will slow down and die soon,' said Ewan. 'I just need to be kept safe for five minutes.'

The door shook as the brothers Earlly shouldered it.

'Five minutes is a long time around here,' said Andrew.

'EWAN!' Amber Feather shouted over the wall. 'There're a lot of people out here who deserve to live. You can do that for them.' Her next sentence started normally but built into a shriek, 'Have some respect *for your ELDERS!*'

May was looking at the Bride's tower. 'Run up to the top,' she said to Ewan. 'That'll buy time. Me and Andrew will keep them back.'

Ewan dashed towards the tower.

THUD.

252

The plantation rocked as Uncle did a five-thousand-tonne bellyflop. The tower seemed to think about it for a few seconds. Then it collapsed before their eyes. It fell in on itself, slumping to the ground and leaving a surprisingly neat pile of masonry and broken woodwork.

Their barricade also collapsed. The old people invaded, five, ten, a dozen of them. Mr Wright grabbed May and hoisted her onto his shoulder. She pounded his back and screamed for Ewan. Others grappled Andrew to the ground. Yesterday, when he was the monster-boy, this would have been impossible. Today they were overpowering him. 'We're sorry about this,' said Mrs Grace. 'But it'll be over soon and I'll make a nice batch of scones.'

Ewan felt something cutting into him. The brothers Earlly had looped him in fishing line. It was thin and transparent but strong. His arms were pinned to his sides and many hands took hold of him.

THUD.

Through the doorway they could see it. Uncle's bulk visible through only a few rows of trees. In the daylight the sacrificed Brides could not be clearly discerned. They were just the darker, denser shapes inside the jelly, like internal organs or the hard bits in jam. The Brides were churned this way and that as Uncle lurched and flattened the next line of pines.

THUD.

Its body could be seen over the top of the wall. Grey patches were appearing on its surface. Uncle was dying. But not fast enough.

'Uncle! Uncle! We love you!'

Some villagers were so overwhelmed by excitement that they dropped to their knees and gave praise to the monster. Amber hit the backs of their heads. 'Don't worship it!' she shouted. 'Feed it!'

The brothers Earlly pulled Ewan towards Uncle. His feet were dragging in the lawn as he struggled. Uncle's arm swung to meet them.

'Unhand him!' came a grand voice. There was a *hissss* of air being run through and the second brother took a blow. Mr Swift was attacking with his cane. Ewan was dropped as the first brother opened his hands. He allowed Mr Swift to smack down on his palms then clamped on the cane and snatched it from him. Mr Swift looked momentarily sad as the brother snapped it in two. Then he rallied, seized Ewan and dragged him away from Uncle's reach. The brothers grabbed Ewan's legs and tugged him back.

THUD.

The broken heap of the Bride's tower shuddered and sank.

Each of Uncle's sproutings was throbbing for Ewan. The hand was in front, snaking through the trees. Streaks of grey cracked and bled wax as the arm stretched. To see Uncle so unhealthy made its worshippers howl with misery.

'Uncle! Uncle! We have a soul for you. Reach for him!'

Mr Swift fought to save Ewan. May forced her captor back until he fell on the tower ruins. Andrew was up too and they both ran to their friend. They should not have come into this compound. It was a dead end and now they had only seconds to escape.

Farmer Able appeared. He stepped onto the lawn. Cradled in his arms was a weapon, an old musket with brass fiddly bits. Mr Swift saw it and laughed.

'Well done, sir!' he exclaimed. 'Sometimes right has to be backed up with threat of force. I hope you can still aim that thing after all these years!'

The three teenagers closed their eyes in the same pained and disbelieving manner. How could Mr Swift be so naïve?

The old farmer raised the musket. 'All I'm aiming to do is live longer,' he said.

Farmer Able shot Mr Swift.

Surprised, Mr Swift crumpled. The brothers Earlly grabbed their sacrifice away from him.

Crackling and jolting, Uncle's hand passed through the doorway. It was sweating small grey pebbles.

May and Andrew grabbed Ewan. Andrew pulled away the fishing line. But Uncle was already here.

255

Ewan took a last look at his friends. 'Don't forget me,' he said.

'Nooo!' May threw her arms around Ewan and clung to him.

Ewan tried to push her off. 'It's me it's after,' he said.

'Yeah, not us,' said Andrew and he threw his big arm around them both. They were winded as he squeezed them tight. *What are you doing?* Ewan would have said if he could have spoken.

Then they were in Uncle's cold hand.

Villagers, the compound wall and tree trucks went by in a gust. The arm was sucked straight back into Uncle's body. Watery flesh splashed on the trio's faces and they were in. A dent like a belly button was left in Uncle's side for a few seconds. It closed with a slurp.

They were inside Uncle.

The teenagers were deep in cold paste. They could feel it swamping their bodies, entering their noses and ears. It pushed into their mouths, force-feeding them its sour oil. There was a deepwater silence, the complete absence of all sound but for bubbling against eardrums. They were sucked upwards. Through Uncle's skin they could see the sky's soft light and the shapes of hills. It was like looking through thick plastic. Uncle's watery flesh made everything blurred. Brides were suspended around them, plugged by Uncle's arteries.

To say Andrew, May and Ewan were frightened would not be accurate. This was beyond fear. Fear ends at such extremes. Their brains just seized up and they were flipped into an almost dull-minded state of acceptance. This was home now. This cold embrace was their new reality. They would have to accept it. Ewan became dusted with phosphorescence. Andrew and May felt a suction try to drag them apart. Uncle was fighting their bond, pouring itself between them. It would have succeeded had it not been for Andrew's big arm, still packed with great strength. He kept them together.

Fizzing began against the arm. Andrew could feel it then see it, grey pollution streaming from his skin and into the swirl of Uncle's innards. He remembered not being able to drink from Lough Linger. The lake had fizzed then too. Andrew's mutation was distasteful to Uncle. That suited Andrew fine. But Uncle was rejecting more than just that. Andrew and May were of the wrong blood type. Uncle could not absorb them. They were incompatible.

The monster could feel the Bride but he was coated in something repulsive. It needed Ewan but could not stand this poison. It reacted. It flipped and crashed, chucking the teenagers up and down. It tried to peel them apart.

Outside, trees bent over as Uncle convulsed and greyed. Its worshippers cried and pounded the ground. Their poor, sick, heartbroken monster.

The three teenagers gripped each other tighter as they barrelled through tunnels of paste. They felt out-crops of rocky hardness scrape at them.

Uncle folded and sucked in on itself.

Wind was dragged through the trees to replace the lost air.

Uncle spat out.

Andrew, May and Ewan spun, globs of fat whipping off them. They crashed and rolled, still hugged to each other. When they stopped they were completely coated in slime and pine needles. Ewan's cheek was pressed into the plantation floor. He opened his mouth and lumps of fatty paste slopped out. His tongue tasted like acid. He could hear Andrew and May coughing up too. He opened his eyes. Centimetres away from Ewan's nose were two pairs of boots. They belonged to the brothers Earlly. Ewan expected to be grabbed and thrown back to Uncle but it did not happen. There was nobody in the boots. Just pebbles.

Uncle solidified. Its innards were lost from sight as its skin turned grey. The Brides and the fish would soon be fossils. The monster was becoming stone. Rows of sproutings hardened to rock pillars. Many snapped at their roots and fell, knocking off others on the way down. The wreckage of stone sproutings built up around Uncle's base. Dust clouded the air.

The villagers did not go around embracing each other or shaking each other's hands. They stood apart to watch Uncle die, each alone. Some cried. Some muttered goodbyes. Some stood. Some stayed on their knees. The teenagers went to Mr Swift's side. He had dragged himself out of the compound and onto the plantation floor to see his work finally done. The musket ball was not so deadly, it was just under his skin. Mr Swift was dying for another reason. His years were catching up with him.

'Listen,' said Mr Swift. He held up his hip flask and gave it a shake. It rattled, the water inside had turned to pebbles.

Andrew took Mr Swift's hand.

'How old are ye?' asked May.

Mr Swift lost interest in the dying monster. He gazed up, as if deciding the sky was a more worthy focus of one's last moments. He thought death was clouding his eyesight and it might have been. But it was also true that real clouds were beginning to roll in over the valley. A pair of swallows glided overhead. Mr Swift followed them with his eyes, unblinkingly, as if having a vision. Their endless summer was over now. These swallows would have to learn to migrate in the winter just like other birds did. 'Imagine!' coughed Mr Swift. 'Swallows live only a few years yet they travel the world, over and back. And then me! Me that's lived so long yet never once left this valley.' He looked at Andrew and gave his hand a weak squeeze. 'But you were worth waiting for,' he said.

Mr Swift crumbled. Stones fell from between Andrew's fingers.

The same thing was happening to the other villagers. Mrs Grace slumped straight down, leaving a pile of rock and cloth. Mr Hume turned to stone from the ground up. When his face hardened, each hair of his white beard sheared away and drifted in the air. Then he cracked open. Farmer Able fell an old man but by the time he hit the ground he was not. His knees shattered and he was rubble. Betty Bird knelt down and curled herself tight, just in time to be turned into a small neat boulder. She did not want to leave a mess.

Back in the village, Mrs Hume was waiting on her garden seat. Her glasses dropped off her face and smashed against her stone lap.

Miss Boswell was in her kitchen. The legs of her chair snapped beneath her weight. She shattered across the tiles.

The Merrimans sat on the ground together. Mr Merriman squeezed Mrs Merriman's hand. He could feel her skin breaking up beneath his fingers and saw a greyness rising behind her eyes. He said, 'Mrs Merriman, it is my plan . . . to forever hold your hand.'

On that spot, two interconnected rocks, both vaguely human-shaped, can still be seen to this day.

Quiet descended on the valley.

Dark spots appeared on the pale granite that used to be Uncle. It was rain. Andrew stood, face up, eyes closed, catching droplets on his face. Andrew loved the rain. Rain was good. May stuck her tongue out to taste it. Ewan caught drops in his hand. They were glad. The only other person left was Amber Feather, still young enough to live without Uncle's aid. She stood among piles of pebbles, her former citizens, and under the shadow of a hill, her former idol.

'That's it,' she said, 'it's all over.' She walked away through the plantation. Andrew, May and Ewan watched her disappear into the rain.

28

In years to come hikers will occasionally walk that hill. They might stop to wonder at some stone pillars joined seamlessly with the granite slope. They will lean against them and have their photographs taken. They will probably wonder at the hill's shape, a near perfectly rounded dome. Weeds, bracken, then bushes and trees will have grown on its lower slopes but the hilltop will be barren. Walking across it will be like walking on a small moon. This hill would not be alone. There would be six in total. No matter how much the hikers ponder the landscape they will not realise that these hills are the dead growths of a monster. The six hills would not be the only remnants. Look at the whole mountain range. The Mountains of Mourne, great rolling domes of granite left behind every time this monster found human company but was one day rejected. The monster's mind will still be there, beneath the mountains, deep deep down. It will be lonely and pushing up again, seeking human company. The hikers might happen upon a spring bubbling from a crack. The water will be crystal clear and smooth. It will be hard to resist.

Six months after the destruction of Lough Linger the paths were overgrown and brambles had burst up through the ruined cottages. Only one building still looked as it did on the day Andrew, May and Ewan first found this valley. The guest house had been the furthest building from the shore and was not damaged. Nor was it abandoned. Two young people lived there.

Ewan took down the heavy cookbook. It opened where it always did, the page where the flower was pressed. It was given to him by a girl named Brigit. He lifted the dry flower, appreciating its lightness against his skin. It was all the inspiration Ewan needed for another afternoon's work. Carefully, he put the flower back in its place. It was safe there – May would probably not open a cookbook for her entire life. Ewan went to mix a bucket of cement.

Soon he was picking his way over boulders and scattered rocks. Once this had been a plantation leading down to a lake. Now it was a crooked gully. At the other end was a bare stone rise. They had named it Uncle's Hill.

It was awkward going. There was no real track. Ewan was carrying the bucket of wet cement. Some was lost to splashes but there was enough for the job. Ewan was looking for something that he had happened upon the day before. Back at the same spot he pushed away some brambles. There it was, a trickle of water coming up through a fissure. Ewan leaned in as close as he dared. The spring smelled fresh. It smelled of crystal and light. It smelled suspicious. He watched as the water rippled unnaturally, lurching towards him.

Ewan poured the cement over the spring. The grey paste bubbled with spring water but more and more weakly as the cement hardened. He fetched some rocks and piled them over it.

Stepping back, Ewan looked at the plug. He knew it was no permanent fix. The water would just rise again somewhere else. He could devote his whole life to stopping its return to the surface and it would still not be enough. Ewan would be gone someday and the monster free to reappear. He would just have to hope that people in the future would be wise to it. In the meantime Ewan would keep it down. That was his plan.

He picked up the bucket and headed home.

Not too far away, May was sitting on a rock slab. The slab was broken at a forty-five-degree angle, sitting against the slope of Uncle's Hill. She rested her chin on her knees and listened to the only sounds she could hear, rain pattering and pines creaking. May was getting used to the quietness. Finally she could understand why people said nature was peaceful. Occasionally she believed it herself, just briefly, until she remembered the truth. Life babbled all the time, digging, hunting, defending, struggling, but nobody could hear it.

Nowadays May was learning to use her eyes.

A young deer sprang across the boulders. It halted the instant it saw the girl, trying to be invisible by stillness. May knew well enough what the deer was thinking. She was just sorry she could not tell it there was nothing to fear. They watched each other. May glanced away and when she looked back the deer was gone.

Time to go home. Andrew was due to visit today. May met her friends on the track and hugged Andrew hello.

'Have you beaten the monster?' she asked Ewan, looking at the empty bucket in his hand.

'Yes,' he said, 'for another day.'

Andrew lived back in their hometown. He gave May a letter from her dad, just like always. 'The forest is getting a hold,' he observed. Moss patches had appeared on Uncle's Hill. Clumps of greenery were taking root around its base.

They walked to the guest house. They still called it the guest house although they were no longer just guests. At the gable Andrew checked on his own handiwork. He had rigged up a set of barrels to collect rainwater. 'Do you get all you need from them?' he asked.

'Plenty,' said Ewan. 'It rains a lot.'

Inside Andrew dropped his backpack, full of supplies, and went to the window. Once this house had a view of a lake but now instead he saw the impassive face of Uncle's Hill.

'We were *in* that,' said Andrew. 'It's still mind-blowing.'

May dropped heavily on the couch. She was normally cheerful when Andrew visited but she was thinking about the deer. She had been nothing special to it, just another person. 'What are we goin' to do?' she asked the boys.

'Eat,' said Andrew. But then he looked at her seriously. May did not mean the next five minutes. She meant next month and next year and the year after that. Both he and Ewan made non-committal expressions. Who knew? Life was full of possibilities but also dangers. You had to mind your step. They had met monsters. They knew the world did not turn on love alone. Ewan would keep the springs down. May had joined the ranks of the ordinary but she would not be ordinary herself, she would always avoid that. One of Andrew's arms hung longer and thicker than the other. It would stay that way, reminding him that he was a champion. Partly at least.

He looked at his fingers and flexed them. 'I don't mind my big arm,' he said. 'In fact, I kinda like it. And I got what I always wanted, to go home.'

'Hooommee,' said Ewan, impersonating Andrew with a smile.

'But now I've realised that I had the wrong idea,' continued Andrew. 'I hadn't worked out what *home* really meant. I was thinking it was a place . . . but really it's people.'

He paused to let them work out what he was saying. May laughed and stretched out, claiming the couch. 'Ye can only sit here when I'm out,' she said.

'She means it,' said Ewan. 'But there's plenty of room. There always has been.'

He pointed to an old certificate, in a frame above the door. Andrew got on his toes to examine it. It was the title deeds of the house. All three of their names were already on it.